THE CYCLOPEAN MISTRESS

Also by Peter Redgrove

The Cyclopean Mistress

SELECTED SHORT FICTION
1960-1990

PETER REDGROVE

BLOODAXE BOOKS

ISBN: 1 85224 207 8

First published 1993 by
Bloodaxe Books Ltd,
P.O. Box 1SN,
Newcastle upon Tyne NE99 1SN.

Bloodaxe Books Ltd acknowledges
the financial assistance of Northern Arts.

Cover printing by J. Thomson Colour Printers Ltd, Glasgow.

Printed in Great Britain by
Bell & Bain Limited, Glasgow, Scotland.

For Penelope and Zoe –
these aids to dowsing and reflection

Acknowledgements

Grateful acknowledgements are due to the following in which many of these short fictions have already appeared: *Ambit, Chelsea Hotel, The Manhattan Review* (USA), *Margin, Memes, Oasis, Poésie Europe, Proposition, Rimbaud Centenary Publication* (Plymouth Arts Centre), *Sulfur, Tenth Muse* and *Verse*; to *Poetry Now* and *The Best of Poetry Now* (BBC Radio 3); and to Routledge Kegan Paul for the author's *The Nature of Cold Weather* (1961), *At the White Monument* (1963) and *From Every Chink of the Ark* (1977).

Contents

III. IN THE ESPLUMEOR

❦ I.

BEETHOVEN OF THE YARD

A Friend

The troublesome subject of my poor friend's face was not his greasy nose nor his streaming brow, not the cheek-clusters of skin eruption like tiny climbing bouquets, nor his great exophthalmia that bulged and winced, nor his chill-prone baldness with stockingette cap, nor his squab stockiness, but a comparatively small section of the band of muscle comprising his upper lip. This was on the right side; if he were surprised, or in the grip of any emotion from anger to gratitude, the odds were that this would twitch, nip, snarl and lift suddenly in a great one-sided ghast. It would tip the chin up with it, and the right eyeball would glare to the ceiling, as if in supplication to some celestial fisher of men who had caught him in the lip with his invisible hook, and was jerking, jerking fit to pull him right off the earth and whisk him up through the ceiling.

I thought it was as Reynolds observed of Dr Johnson when painting his portrait, that the twitches, gasps and head-jerkings the portraitist desired to cease, could be controlled: it was as though they were knowledge of sins and motion of apology to the Doctor's God, and he could store up the necessity, so to speak, and leave them accumulated until another time. But my friend was not a humble man; it was as though he were in truth being fished from above, against his conscious desire, and a handicap additional to all the other gifts of his appearance, he would say.

Because it really seemed to him to come from above, as it looked, in glaring upwards he often remarked that the ceiling felt to him like a surface, white because it reflected light downward, and concealing the upper air in the same way as the pond-surface is a wriggling mirror to the fish. 'One day he'll get me, and it'll look like a stroke. But it'll be me dancing in the air and kicking my heels through the ceiling all the same. Straight upwards, and I shall wonder how long the line is,

11

how far I shall fall upwards until I see my fisherman. I had a nightmare the other night in which he not only looked like me, but he had this very same trouble with his lip, because he was the prey of a greater fisherman still, with a still longer line upwards, and he with a trouble in his lip too, and for the same reason, and so on. And then suddenly the heavens cleared and I saw them all, one above the other, fishing each other, receding, not to infinity, but curving as they receded, encircling the curved universe, and returning beneath my feet. So when I looked down I saw that I was a fisher of gods.'

Thus my poor friend. Then he had fantasies of eating and being eaten, and would doodle all day fishes with their tails in their mouths. I saw him walking along in the park, twirling his umbrella, and his eyes were on the great circle whirled out by its ferrule, and his clothes were shining with the rain. I think he caught his death by some such piece of absent-mindedness, for he went into a fever, and nothing could be done. I hurried to his bedside, but I was too late.

His mother had been there, and as I reached the top of the stairs she came hurrying out of the bedroom door. Her eyes were shining and I thought at first he'd recovered. 'No,' she said, 'he's dead. But the last thing he said was '"Mother, the chain is broken"'.'

Lake Now-and-Again

A bird cried out like a cracking stick; I blushed and pulled up my trousers...

We had passed an empty cottage with a window open on a neatly turned-down bed and a quiet and dusty grandfather clock...

And afterwards we felt that the sounds of our romp had reached the smarmy ears of the worms cramped like white knitting in the underturf caves – they knew – the bird that snapped out at us as we were getting up knew – so did the skeletons flouncing up to the dark altars in the drowned cathedral deep in the lake whose banks shook at our vehemence...

And if the blue sky-gods knew they would stoop down suddenly and sip up all the water in a great whirling funnel to expose us, the skeletons collapsed in the ooze, peering up sagely through the tiny lakes of blue water caught in their eye-sockets, the knowing worms looping away into the mud, skulls piled like rocks, our secret place filled with a sudden silent audience...

And we ran, still gripping hands...

And there was a little carriage empty and quiet in the lane, the travellers gone off to set up a lakeside fête – their horses respectful enough, jingling the harness mildly now and then – gone to rehearse the band – bang and pipe – (and the lake suddenly flies up to the sky, leaving cliffs and a towering weedy lump in the middle which was a cathedral, water gushing out of the sides and the great rotted west door bursting open mingled with candlesticks and long bones, our parents – proud helpers! – and the mayor himself staring down into the glossy recesses – the comedians striking up with satirical music: they would nod at each other, knowing who was responsible – and jingle back in conference...)

...still running...down the hill we went, out of the wood, pretending they were pounding after us to make us marry, all of them, the gallop of heel-bones, laughter like smashed dishes, sacramental goblets fast-rusted to chest-bones – pretending till panic took us and we ran like maniacs, scattered pebbles and twigs snapping up at our ankles...

...out of the trees into the open lane where the sky bore down on us with a blue world-wide stare...

But it was sleepy with lids of rain, and we got away scot-free while the lake filled up and pressed down, was made good – ourselves back at our two homes eloquently excusing our absence, refreshed, drenched and free – until the next time, in a new place.

The Cyclopean Mistress

'A man is a god in ruins...' This sentence was written beneath a musical stave in black on a greenboard. A poster of skeletons hung on a nail. An old photograph taped to the stationery cupboard showed a sculptor in a smock, with a noble brow and the expression of a Caesar; in his left hand he held the limp mask of an idiot, clay-hued and rubbery. Several diplomas in frames hung on the wall. I thought them more appropriate to a private office; the teacher's qualifications were not in question. I had been told that she had only one eye...

But I was not prepared for the teratism that walked in, her schoolmaster gown billowing. This one had no need of expedients to control her fourth-formers! Indeed she had one eye, but it was in the centre of her forehead, an inch above the bridge of her nose. She made me feel quite alcoholic with the buzz of it.

Once I had got used to the cyclopean feature, the rest had great beauty. The hair was raven black, and flowed like some perfumed and healing balsam down to her shoulders. Her skin was clear and glowing, her figure lissom, her movements quick, agile and intelligent. I had come to enquire about my daughter's progress in school. What the Cyclopean mistress told me was 'She is well towards approaching unified vision.' I could see that she weighed her words, but I wonder what this phrase meant for the future of my child? Would her eyes fuse, too, and crown her nose?

I had expected an older woman with a handsome black patch, like Wotan's. Then I thought of Ancient Greece, and wondered whether the schoolmistress was a classical scholar? Was she, with her Eye, the offspring of the Beginning, when Earth coupled with the Sky? I had read about her three one-eyed brothers in Homer, and in Hesiod how they made thunderbolts for Zeus. But I had not heard rumour of a daughter of that coupling. If a god of this kind were ruined – how? –

would the eyeball not split in two and drop down into divided sockets on either side of the nose, leaving nothing of that unified vision but a worried frown?

Strong Sugar

A good catch of pilchard meant money, meat and light all together in one night – the whore pleased – having served the meat, snuffed out the fishoil lamp – and thus many males and females lie together for money in the same shoal after that catch.

We are a poverty-culture, as Japan used to be. Civilisation satisfies itself with contemplation of flowers, and insects within the flowers, gorgeously inhabited. But it is better not to wander far at night from your bed or the brown dusk of your house in the circular village thatched like hives and within each at the centre the woman's hearth, the bright bees of fire swarming there, and the wood in the hole, the door shut.

Every night there was a birthday, somebody was bound to have a birthday among all those visitors, so each night in her great hut we gathered round the cakes, the amphiphontes, the round shiners; there was always a birthday until the burial of our chief, then there was a funeral. Our first death – would you believe it? She was buried in a tun of dry sugar; a browner stain moved slowly into the amber crystals, and she dried in a year to a fragrant corpse light as basketwork. She made strong sugar, the whore who civilised and loved us.

They call us the Sweet Ones. Even in the pouring rain our clients having done their flaps up and tidied themselves generally, pause to marvel at how the little wood fills them with reflections, partly its rainy look, partly the scent of wet tree-buds growing, and at the sooty beehive floating above made of millions of humming drops with one bright sting as it lightens. They are so sweetly at peace that they themselves are like insects within the encompassing flower of hills, waterfalls and the ever-moving clouds, gorgeously inhabited.

Beethoven of the Yard

Beethoven of the Yard, his eyes shining with lust and romance; he is the senior catcher. The height of his collar and the depth of its opening indicate how essential to his craft is the smell of his chest as it pants after its prey. Here is the secret of intuition! The smell of his bosom perceived by dipping his chin in his romantic collar answers his queries about his quarries; the perfume of his chest swiftly changes and he knows the man is innocent! Even in the driving rain his raincoat is open to the breastbone, it is his inner light as the glistening capes of the constable guard the bloody corpse whose fluids wash away down the rosy gutters; he pulls the brim of his hat down and stares at the paving stones for an answer, the hairs on his chest tangling with his hirsute nostrils; a rising smell of daffodils and blood answers him and he knows it was the nurseryman who slaughtered his victim and slashed him to pieces by tossing him through the greenhouse glass into the early flowers before dragging him back to the street and the gutter. Slowly he raises his finger like a conductor's baton and points 'Thou art the man!' Now Beethoven von Hound wends his way to his solitary bedsit, the day's crimes identified by their individual fragrance. But fragrances are not accessible to memory. One must meet the presence. One must be up promptly the next day searching for early morning crimes, fresh with the dew.

My Shirt of Small Checks
(My BBC Shirt – Ronnie Corbett)

I. *The Listener*

And the radio said: 'I will be a little sanctuary unto them.'

It is a little sanctuary among the hills in the desolation of winter.

Invisible rays tumble over the hills and through the hills like a stiff breeze of watered silk that we cannot see.

Minerals in the hills glow for an instant: Doris? says Dan Archer, Doris? A whisper in the mine galleries, Dan? are you there?

I believe that the madman can receive all these rays in his head at one blort. His sanity depends on the degree to which he can differentiate Cliff Michelmore motoring over the wide sands from the vultures of the nine o'clock news that have gathered dispersing the macaws of Woman's Hour among the doves of the previous night's Epilogue; meanwhile the golden eagle of a budget broadcast flies slowly and heavily into the full round setting sun of Desert Island Discs. The madman stands under his palm tree unable to switch off the birds or the sunset or Cliff Michelmore. Oil from Wheelbase spreads across the incoming tide like a supple breeze of watered silk.

'Let Broadcasting House declare an amnesty and a cease-fire,' cries the madman, as the Open University flows over his head, 'for there is only noise where there should be silence! My talent,' he cries, 'was to tune into the silence as I wished, to the sea, to the whale-song and dolphin sonar-talk (in which illumination counts for less than transparency!); to the white crests of the sizzling ionosphere; to the moon as it flies overhead pulling babies out of mothers and dying persons out of their own gasping mouths, its strata bowing against strata, like an orchestra of violins; to the endless warm broadcasts of the sun that feed us all,' the madman says. 'Why, as the sun goes down, BBC2 rises, and passes across the heavens, and sometimes does not set until one o'clock the next morning.'

As for myself, I am no madman. My transistor is a block of singing minerals, and I wish their changes were visible to me, and as they gave me Uncle Vanya on Radio Four, I could watch the slow-blooming sparks through a transparent cabinet, the hour-glasses of transparent sands, the shifting spectra deep inside the instrument like the flashes of light off innumerable alert pince-nez, that turn into Chekhov's spoken words.

I regard this instrument as the hybrid of a choir and a mine, or something between a church and a factory, or an offspring of the Houses of Parliament and the Research Division of ICI.

The cabinet-minister voices stride up and down its embassy stairs as I lie in the darkness visualising the salt woollen smell of their suits, the rain glittering on their taut umbrellas, the manly leather dispatch cases.

In the morning, a fly listens with me in the kitchen to Yesterday in Parliament. It returns again and again to the one spot on the transistor-cabinet, which I guess is transmitting information – perhaps a taste merely, or a sexual impulse – on a frequency beyond my capacity. I guess that this complex stone may have many different messages for the whole of the animal kingdom. I shall set it down in the midst of a rabbit-warren, I shall trawl it through the oyster-beds. The bacteria that alight on it and breed in the grease of my fingermarks pass through three generations during the course of Midweek Theatre, and who knows what powers of mutation A Book at Bedtime may possess.

My wireless drinks the sharp salt taste from the nipples of its batteries. As I replace the drained cells I pull a small curtain aside and gaze on the formal garden of coloured wires and soldered blobs, the sigil-scaffolding that strains music from all the other forces of the atmosphere, the musical intoxicant prepared from crushed air.

I am too gross to enter this garden until I have eaten a small cake. Who in Broadcasting House keeps a supply of these small cakes?

II. *His First Broadcast*

I remember how a certain old man who had never in his life broadcast, died in this house, whistling all its symphonies back over the air into his radio-set. Now I sit in the kitchen, the fleece-white letter of acceptance in front of me, glowing with its red ranch-brand Twinbee Sea.

When I am broadcast, I shall be changed into a complex vibration that is neither living nor dead. I shall travel up and down the broad stairs of coloured sands in company with the voices of prime ministers.

Whether you listen to me or not, I travel through you and your apartments. Deep in the hills, the mines speak. 'Redgrove,' they whisper, 'Peter? A poem by Peter Redgrrrr...' and the beam wanders growling.

For a mere twenty-five minutes or so a line of black bats from Poetry Now perches on a white tree of static. I am one of them.

George MacBeth has given me the small cake to eat and I enter the garden of transistors and singing mineral flowers. Now I should learn also how to travel into the mirrors of every household, but for this knowledge I shall have to go to the noiseless dead poets, and to my friend who died mad from the radio in his head and who daily scratches broadcasts into my own skull, mirror-lined.

Riding Crocodiles in Falmouth

By the immortal childhouse, or Saxon Cross, the quick wake of crocodiles. 'Look at it, my 'ansome, they'm cutting it down – that ol' tree, Oh I knows 'e's rotten – but they'm killing the history.' The tall green canopies like the quick wakes of crocodiles, the scaly trunks diving into their dividing foliage.

The grandchild infant sleeps pale and fat in her shawl. The hail-shower, clicking along the tiles, dragging its leash, scratching itself, makes all the restless dog-noises of a hailshower. The crib has deep ruffles. The cloud banks build up but are blown away as swiftly. The sun lights up the whitewashed walls of the outhouses blindingly.

New buds are already full and green, comforting to her. A sparrow comes hopping for crumbs of her breakfast, it is large and strong and the colour of an old schoolbook she remembers. It clings on to the fence with hooked claws like a wonderful deliberate machine and whirls off as an outhouse door bangs.

The trees lash their tails, tugging at the earth. They are green as crocodiles diving upwards with something in their teeth, they are elms, coffin trees, green consumers. There is a bird-table in the lilac tree; sparrows, blue-tits, wrens tug at the reticule of nuts; the blossom is a big flowering show or cinema against the whitewash; the breathing tree-blouse patterned with birds in the street-theatre of the boughs.

The friend with her grumbling arrives and drinks a cup of tea while the birds all fly away. The show stops, resumes when she has gone. The field of ooze by the river is greening already, and there is an immortal childhouse in the churchyard, a stone cross, a childsize Jesus nailed to its tree; two small birds perch on it, their heads flicking and flashing each way. The cinema of lilac flickers across the whitewash and its starring scents reach out in 3D.

Now the sky changes. The foliage darkens to lead everywhere, but especially in the churchyard where the dead hold their breath. Now the hail rattles down on the roofs and on the immortal childhouse and snuffles between the tombs like dogs hunting; the white ice rolls; there is a smell of freezing metal; the hailflints spark their freezing fire; then the sun warms, and the ponds are Egyptian waters.

The Model

The birds sing a particularly learned song in the apple trees, and the passive stars within those fruit shine through their skins. This is how she prepares for the art school hours. She is to be five hours nude, the life-room model, so she has brought her little Walkman to play the learned birdsong to herself through headphones like a stethoscope, and they allow her to eat one of her own apples providing she eats unmoving. The storm wheels a mile over her model's canopy throne.

Nude, she is implored by the young fast-working pencils to prolong her untransforming look, but the sky gathers along the high voltage of its curdling surfaces from which pour waterfalls, both visible and audible, rattling on the skylight; invisible and inaudible 'fluences, sferics and atmos stride into the high-ceilinged studio noticed only in so far as they move the work beyond reasonable comprehension.

The electric lights are giddy from the storm, and in its tension these young artists find themselves wishing to paint a nimbus, halo or penumbra radiating from her flesh, for it is there.

Their pencils are like aerials of black lightning; the storm breaks its washes down and is coming through as a woman's form with legs like two very long flights of steep stairs into the thunder. But as it recedes like flying granite or floating mines that dynamite themselves and pour new chasms of water, she changes back into a harmless nude.

How will they now account for the apparitions manifest on their easels? The mountainous staircases, the black eggs shattering with yolk-gold lightning, the gargoyles with their look of disembowelling thunder, the cathedralled gates of cloud through which pass winged cowls of angels whose every feather is a face?

Unanswering, the enthroned nude eats her everlasting apple; the orchard-birds resume their learned commentary, tingling her ears only, in the tiny Walkman.

After the Flood

I looked down through the floodwater at the sunken boat. The windowsill of my bedroom was rough and damp; the water lapped to within six inches of it. I craned out and saw the boatman's corpse bobbing in its cloud of little nipping fishes. I had heard over the transistor that nobody had yet come to rescue the dead from their inappropriate graves, inaquated rather than inhumed; the living were still marooned, as I was.

Cilla was taking her turn on the roof-parapet, waving the sheet. We had spread one out on the tiles and tied another flapping from the television aerial, which had shivered all night and howled, like the skeleton ghost of a monkey. I thought I would join her, and was about to slosh back again over the carpets and upstairs through the attic, when I heard a dull boom that came from under my feet. I stared across the water; a white plume was collapsing back into a far surface like a felled snow tree. Sliding towards me over the water was a small black shape, which paused for a moment, and then rowed on. Another boom, another plume. I looked down over my sill into the water; now it was shivering-full of sooty fish big as boots. I looked at their working mouths; they had come for us.

The boat came rowing over our garden. I hailed it: 'Hello! Have you come to rescue us? We have just enough paraffin to boil you some tea.' As I spoke, a plume of water reared itself by the elms waist-high in water at the gate. The man in the boat was bearded, and quite old. Between his feet there was an open case of dynamite, shining brown sticks in white dusty packing. 'Why are you dynamiting?' I asked. I helped him across the sill through the open window. His coat was marked Sussex C.C. across the back. 'Instructions,' he said, 'I'm dynamiting at about 100 yard intervals along the submerged roads. To keep the drains free.' 'Will you row us to the town? First light in the morning?' 'Yes. I'll not dynamite any more. First time a lot of potatoes came up. Among them a policeman's helmet. I fished it out. Look down into the water.' I looked. With the twilight a faint pulsing glow had come into the depths against which the fishes hung and darted like drops of sentient ink. 'I think I broke a gas-main with my second shot. Something caught on fire in the water. Look over towards the Leats.' About a mile distant a red hot dome of fire quaked and shone just below the surface, like an underwater mosque burning.

How Much For the Box?

'What do you make of this?' asked the antique-dealer. The second-hand books rose like stale autumn forests around him. On the table was a leather case, bound with straps and buckles. It was black, and though dusty and worn, was made of the sort of soft leather that could take a high polish, and had once done so. Its look said 'custom built'.

'Shall I undo it?' He nodded. I began to unbuckle the straps. The surface crackled a little as I pushed them back: the leather had got dry from lack of attention. The cover was hinged, and creaked as I opened it.

Inside the case was a slab of ebony: black, polished wood. Set in a hollow of this was a silver object, conical, resembling a pear, or perhaps a stylised heart. There was an opening in the front of this object: it was hollow, and lined with a fine red velvet.

I looked at the dealer. He nodded again. I picked up the silver pouch, turning it round, looking at my reflection in the bright, slightly tarnished metal. 'What is it?' 'Blamed if I know,' said the dealer, 'there are some keys too. Look.' The ebony slab was also hinged, and behind it a recess. In the recess, like the false bottom of a suitcase, there was a transparent packet of long, spiky-looking keys. 'Skeleton keys, these are,' said the dealer. He picked them up and shook them out of the packet to show me. There was also a piece of folded paper. I picked this up. It was a heavy vellum, and there was something stuck to it, hard and crackling, like mucilage, in a patch, like dried fish-skin. 'This is a caul,' I said. 'Some babies are born with this skin over their heads. It's supposed to be very lucky, a charm against drowning. The child is often said to become a seer. There's something written on the paper.' The ink was green, and the writing scrawling. I could not make out the word. At first I thought it said 'adytum' then 'adman' or 'atman' or 'lumen'. 'Look at this, though,' said the shopkeeper, opening the remaining fold in the paper. The top of it was crested with an embossed portcullis and the legend 'House of Commons'. 'What'll you give me for it? Curious, eh?' I held the silver pouch, or fig, or heart. It was pleasantly warm and rounded to the touch. 'It's a bit ghostly,' I remarked, 'but no more, I suppose than anything else in the shop.' There came a tapping at the window. I looked round and saw Elsa beckoning to me. A taxi was drawn up at the kerb. Elsa had my ticket and was tapping on the window with it. 'Sorry, I must go. I'm expected in London. Business.' I thought of how my "business" would look to antique-dealers in the future, though it was of a size to interest archaeologists first. I sell particle-accelerators: cyclotrons and the like. We site them like spiral shells or dancing-grounds in remote parts of the world, and we torture matter into electricity inside them. I wished I had a gentler craft. Perhaps one day I would take up a new hobby: devising puzzling and equivocal antique objects. In the meantime I was in the business of making the universe stream through mirror-corridors and tunnels, making it turn odd corners, and break usual rules. How did an electron beam feel as it prickled through a cloud-chamber, or irradiated my mountains of metal? That was not the sort of question that sold particle accelerators, I said to myself, as I thought of how my thoughts had sped on round my head between lifting one foot and putting it down again, walking towards Elsa's black hair and whitish face behind which the human particles moved in sentient street-patterns, through a soft forest of books, wood that had been irradiated with print particles still until they started thoughts whirling, among the mirror tunnels of the street's shop-windows. And if I slowed down, if my particles moved at the speed of, say, lead, then this street and this town and this girl would flicker like the flames of a fire, or the tracings of particles in my machinery. If I slowed down the events in the accelerators, or speeded up the recordings of the collisions, build-ups, fusions, cohesions, fissions of these impalpable particles, might I see trees, shops and houses living their lives within my machines? I think this between the putting down of this foot, and the picking up of that, in a fast walk towards Elsa, who is tapping slowly on the window.

On an impulse I stopped, and turned. 'How much for the box?' 'A fiver,' said the dealer. 'Right.' I tucked it under my arm. Perhaps it was a machine for creating thoughts of this kind.

The Moment

The briefcase was light yellow in colour, with broad stitching along its margins and fastenings, and a clasp of brass-coloured metal. It sat solidly on the speckled composition floor in the recess of the newsagent's kiosk entrance in the round hall of Leicester Square underground station. At eleven o'clock in the morning it was between rush-times, and there were only a few people around. He looked up from the case across the whitely-lit hall to where the escalators descended into their bright gulfs. Over there the stairs from the street entered their arches, and the Moss Bros window displayed its stuffed, headless shirts.

This was the moment of Russian Roulette. Was the briefcase loaded? The public had been warned to report any luggage left in public places, for terrorism was in the air. Posters everywhere proclaimed the danger. Whereas once it was a graphic picture of a hurrying train a door of which some fool had opened, ready to sweep an innocent mother and child along the platform, now it was fire and shrapnel leaping from the corner of a crowded station concourse at a variety of innocent passers-by. England blandly ignored the pain of other people's politics; England must be made to feel.

But England did not feel, any more than it felt during the war. It coped, or seemed to cope, or muddled through. Posters went up, the public felt itself united against a common enemy. England comported itself by means of caricatures and cartoons of attitudes; it walked its tightropes.

Thus, he thought, his madness was explained. There was no reason why he should not report the case. There was every reason why he should not touch it. Did he want to be dead, or crippled? He could not imagine such a thing. What nightmares, what revised images of himself did the briefcase contain? It did not look like a case stuffed with death-warrants, but it might be. Militating against its being a bomb, was its light colour and its plain visibility, and the fact that it was made of decent leather. Militating for, was the observation that nobody was likely to leave behind such a case deliberately, or to place it in such an exact manner.

He took hold of the clasp, and carefully undid it. He was ready to open the mouth of the case. In the next second he would see – some papers, some apples, a banana, a packet of sandwiches. Perhaps he would see a neatly-folded pair of pyjamas, a night-dress tucked into the opposite compartment, a towel and a spongebag in the middle section; a happy case left by lovers too full of each other to be mindful of their lovers' properties.

He opened the case. He heard a click, like a metallic bar falling, like a lock opening. Then the lions and the lionesses were ripping off his clothes and biting his bones and he dwindled beneath them until he went out.

The ticket collector was knocked off his stool, and glass tinkled in a powdery form like snow all over his body. In the ticket kiosk, the clerk was standing stunned, money in his hand. Ticket-machines were thrown down, and one of them went on carefully printing out 20p yellow tickets with magnetic strips down their backs. After the roar, there was no sound. Everything happened in silence and slow motion: the bang of the explosion had deafened, and the emergency had speeded up everyone's life. Everyone's except the man who had opened the case. He had been flung against a wall, which was splashed with a great blot of his blood, like an octopus hanging on the wall behind him, and sliding down it with dangling arms. The ticket-collector hauled himself on to his feet, brushed at the white dust with large black hands. Several people appeared at the entrances to the street. A policeman walked forward, very carefully, over towards the corpse. Bending, he made as if to pick up a piece of yellow ragged leather, then thought better of it – it was evidence. He looked at the shallow scorched crater by the shattered kiosk. He went on towards the sprawling body, felt for a pulse under the ear. The blood that should have been there glittered on the wall. 'Quite a small one, Sarge,' commented the pulse-feeling policeman to the other uniformed officer who was approaching, 'why will they do it?'

Army of Mice

I woke up gasping. I had somewhere in a dream lost my breath, and losing my breath, lost the dream, and trying to breathe woken myself up. It was a nightmare. I could remember no succubus sitting on my chest. I had not been twined in intercourse with any bestial figment. But then I started remembering my dream. In my dream I had been asleep, and I woke. I began to sit up, and to adjust the eiderdown. It shivered and squeaked under my grasp and I understood that the quilted coverlet was composed of the bodies of living mice. I looked down at the bedding which covered me, and I saw that it was studded like a city night with yellow eyes. I tried to throw it off, but it parted to my hands, and then came surging up at me. I flung myself out of the bed and my feet touched cold stone flooring. I tried to find my slippers. A pair of slippers stood under the bed. I tried to pick them up, and they were mice. I touched the lampshade on the bedside table and tried to find the switch, but it was the tiny teeth of mice, and the whole table gleamed with eyes.

My feet touched a carpet. It wriggled and clasped me with its teeth. It was mice. I took my dressing-gown from behind the door and put it on. My body gleamed with the eyes of mice. The dawn began to come up and showed me clothed in grey fur, covered in eyes. I pulled the curtain. Mice that had been clinging to mice by claw and fur, tail and teeth to make the warm heavy drapes, left hold and dropped to the floor in hundreds to let the thin dawn light into the room. I looked at the soft grey clouds in the sky, and they opened all their sparkling eyes and were mice. I felt my face with my hand: it was covered with a soft stubble like mouse-fur, and as I touched it it wriggled and I passed my hand between mice. I looked at my hand and my hand looked at me out of mice-eyes, I looked back at it out of my face of mice-eyes, and the room became gradually taller and broke up into thousands upon

31

thousands of identical rooms as my head broke up and began to run on mouse-claws down over my body which was running away over the floor to all four corners of the room.

Cold University

I accompanied the Prussian Army as the curator of its War Museum. They created relics of themselves in plenty, of themselves and others on their destroying marches through the massed Teutonic snows. Like a sleety beachcomber I followed after.

Later, the King donated white palaces which could be used as universities for the study of Atomic Ice. The study, for example, of the pure round-sound of falling ice which brings a chill to the whole earth and topples with a pure whisper which is at the same time six-sided,or of the sky full of sky falling and the rivetting of hail, the tattoo of curdled dew on the iron roof, like snare-drums that are made of cold so white because it is silver, and that is because of the blue in it which is made of creamed piles of radio despatches that have splashed with the clatter of routed cavalry across our VDUs out of the floating cumulus universities that are being shelled to pieces, and the shuttered salons shattered by the thunder; or to study the freshly-new-each-time smell in the air of ice falling, the theory being that the moon has been photographing in its silver our to-and-fro night-battles, and has shed its films from the innumerable pocks of its meteoric scar-tissue, and is floating clear and unblemished as an empty plate above the snow that is falling from its clearing face and which is composed of these pictures of us killing each other and our horses.

At any rate, war has dissolved in the air and is crystallising. Each flake is different, yet a perfect two-legged, two armed and single-phallused soldier in frost, with hailstone eyes and epaulettes of ice; each one a graduate of the palace rolling above, the university of pinnacles that has learnt to fly. It is the King's University in which his Infantry study to pass out with a contagious degree communicated by these cold soldiers capable of ubiquity; all around they land with their swords out – but the chill passes straight through the skin without benefit of cutlass.

33

Writing a Play for Radio and Children

Let the nib that writes the task be like an aerial broadcasting, the ink like a triacle of life, a medicinable treacle, and the paper a white camphor, broadcasting presence.

The chubbiness of the moon! and under it the snowman with his bottles of moonshine, his thousands of flakes smashing light white, in every direction, powdering light as in a mortar. The Child's Prize Snowman, a blank floating county of snow compressed into mansize, a one cloud compressed and in its human or semi-human shape neverthelessless retaining altitude, that faint blueness in the white. Now we are in the presence of a sky that is falling in gentle dabbing pawmarks.

The task keeps time, for the ticking of his eight whitefaced clocks synchronises in climaxes each midnight, and draws apart once more. The nib splits its back and goes on spitting black or differentiating the white, and for that one instant I saw a black snowman with white shining eyes, where's he gone! as midnight shakes the room with clocks and at twelve a.m. the timepieces strike together with appalling unanimity, but at noon they take one hour precisely to complete their course of chimes. And noon exactly overhead discloses that the Children's Mine is full of flowers, to the brim of its shaft, rust red flowers, for where the old mines had been worked a lofty sunbeam sinks perfectly upright into bottomless diggings.

And the stones in the churchyards lean like grey figures putting their heads together to decide about the past, and lose their shadows, which withdraw into the stone. Shadows withdraw into the hill of dew and spiderweb, of gauze which is one entire web; and its spiders withdraw behind it in the noon, for the sun is risen in these lenses; and the cow, exalted by milking, walks in shadowless air.

How can I write a play in such a noon when with the shadow gone (which may well be the play) the senses cram together in, for instance, that flower with one big pistil at its centre whose shape is like the belling of a pail to a spurt of milk, a living nib. That flower and that milky memory light a path and so we feel it would usefully inspire to invest my jade nib into her perfumed mouse and enter the scented garden that is within…but such a scene would make the tassels writhe, and that would never do, not in the echoing mine of Radio 4, the Children's Mine. Then as this quarry is full of its red flowers, into her Infant Girl again, her Red Pearl, her Precious Stone, down between the Strings of her Guitar.

At the finish it always seems that their precious soul has fled. That is temporary. It returns perfumed, broadcasting its single presence like that triacle, like that milky camphor in the flower's basking knob. How can I now call that other task sweet?

The Wedding by the Powerhouse

The salt, the little loose mixture, the saint's bowl of salt, for the circle, without which he will not sing; the small loose mixture finely crystallised like a free-flowing song; some bone-ash, a little pinch of death, keeps it freely-running, except

By the powerhouse it clings, the crystal windows stuck down with electricity because of the great wheels thundering inside, because of the wide cables rooting underground; he will not sing without this bowl, it is his instrument by which he knows what other powers are present, what immense generated footprints tangle their magnetism through the long grass.

The audition seats were a grassy bank. His body had a fourfold voice; his heart had many kinds of pulse in a freely-flowing mixture, as in the Chinese system.

As he sings, the skin clarifies like melting butter, or as the clouds slide off the sun, opening the world to every feeling. I swear he sung the clouds away, accompanying himself on his different pulses, holding their harmony,

thus the tuned circuitry of two clouds hummed and they prepared to make thunder, but, with a chord sung in his four-fold mode, he drove them together with a melodious twang and the rain pelted down on the wedding party, whose electricity was thus discharged – and so they were able to complete the ceremony in perfect fitting calm, by the powerhouse on the banks of the green river, by virtue of the singer, Constanter, the Singer, his salt-bowl damp.

I was present at his birth.

He sang himself out of his Mother, his Mother pulled herself off his head, which shone with grease and blood and un-muffled song.

He sang at his own wedding, in the pouring rain, the bride dressed as a waterfall, the electricity gone into the ground and replaced by song;

and all the saints glowed in their clouds and in their window-glass as he sung his son out of his wife, the ship down the greasy slipway, and his mistress out of her remarkable blouse.

Car Drives Light

In Cornwall they live on copper and fish and tin – each of these commodities has a shiny skin. As they go for their walks they take turns to sing, turning round and round in the moon's radiance (which is thunder reversed at the other end of the sky), while the motions of the schools of fish, the subterranean motions of the ore, why, they are only caused by the love of God and the lunar tides. One thin copper penny sets the wheel of fortune turning.

They pluck the car's engine out to manufacture electric light from the churning of oil-buttery metal; the brilliant lamps dangle from their black flex, their dark webs of unmanifested electricity. The dark lines make the bright ones shine.

The old barn with the rafters alive in their parks and groves of the small forestry of moss – it is their powerhouse. Even before they installed the engine in its new capacity as generator they relished the slaty perfume from the broken tiles, the bouquets of the nettles pushing through the fallen roof; and the rafters resurrected to forest life by moss and wetrot were thinly luminous in the darkness of the hovel, traced in its twilight blue meridians above, before the barn became this furnace of light in the stink of petrol.

He said he felt like a needle tuned to the skies, a metal tuned to the stars. The old engine coughed to start, then ran smooth. The light poured out of its dirty hulk, invisible until it reached the lamps; its rust-clogged sides were like a meteor fallen millions of years ago and still generating, still inspiring light, which poured from the broken barn like an extraordinary harvest overflowing. Their skins were radiant, every broken straw was a golden pipe, the cobwebs gold thread and sharp shadow –

light pouring from old metal and liquid rock with a smell like burning shells, the pistons working as they should for the love of God. The cable snakes into the house, looking for places to put its light. Now we shall cook and run our radios on this light.

They turn transistors on all over the house, boulevards of music, paths of heart, ways through the ear to the gentle lands, and this drowns the noise of the petrol engine.

Mood

It is a plum tree shivering like a ghost. The mood darkens, the blue sky darkens, the misty plums darken, the thunder bends over as a black nanny bends over a cot. The fool throws his bike into the lake and claps his hands in joy as the angular difficult machine disappears. There is an alteration in the air like a staircase forming. The fool is interested in one round dew condensed in the canoe of a leaf at eye-height. Within it the whole scene is held. Then he pushes out his lips and eats it. He waves his arms and blinks his eyes and looks as if he is struggling awake.

Then the rain crashes down. The fool is caught in his mother the rain. He shines with her glory. He is deafened with her downpour. Then he crosses into the small wood and the rain-sounds recede to the pattering on green roofs. The paths through the wood are as lacy as his mother's nightdress. She died in it and they had to unravel all the lace to let her ghost escape. The rain has penetrated the labyrinth of his own clothes now, and in their chill everything he sees touches him. The trees make a great hand to touch him. A black rabbit under a hazel tree stands up and begs as he passes; he hands it a small rainsoaked piece of sandwich.

He preferred the train to the bike engloutie. He felt that he had turned the earth itself, all the way from Exeter to Falmouth. The journey was so long and busy in the rattling coaches joined end to end. Each moment shook earth off the spade. He passed villages the water had partly devoured and laid out in Colosseums of mudflat. He was certain that he passed safe harbours where in underwater palaces there was secret teaching. One station with factories behind was as white as marble temples.

He slides another canoe-full of rain to the back of his throat, and steps out again into the meadows. Immediately Eros the serpent desire flew through the air and the electrical clouds began altering his mind again, opening it sometimes as if in answer to prayers, sometimes slamming it shut, leaving it bruised, balsamic and bloody. He looks round for something else it can conjure instead of him, plants his walking-stick, strolls away.

Moon Rising Over Richmond Park

There is a young deer crowned with a wreath of mist standing stock-still at the coppice-edge. It turns and merges with the trees, suddenly invisible, like a soul of the trees. It is a deer that stands like a portal in the coppice, still as a door, ready to turn, and turns, flashing its scut, springing and melting through the moiré boles. She quit her darkness and stood at the margin of trees as the coppice breathed deeply and stretched towards the rising moon whose beams slice deeply round its contours. Now it loosens and floats free. This was the reason the deer paused at the brink, sniffed at the thinning air as the island of earth continued to rise, and returned. The voyaging shadow of the mountain of earth and trees and deers darkens the city. In the chasm created by its absence the little silver springs begin to construct a lake. Astronomers in the city exclaim at the shadow on the moon, which reveals itself in the telescope to be a gracious park.

The entire park returns as the moon sets and settles again into its crater, an exact fit. It flew with a just-audible hiss of leaves across the sky, great roots dangling from it like an under-forest, and it left a track of perfume broad as a prairie.

Perfumeuse

Now in the morning she practises on the piano, the notes play in their turn upon her incense; the piano-music reverberates in her premenstrual perfumes which are the true lunar incense; these perfumes are absorbed by the books and stand upon the shelves within their pages as in a pharmacy of stopped bottles full of odorous magisteries, ready for use. Take a title down and open its pages, read and inhale! be inspired by the faintly-perfumed piano-music. When the full moonbeams strike through the french windows spirit rolls off these shelves like full bolts of silk thrown down unrolling along a draper's counter, with a gasp of astonishment at the colour and the smoothness – in that gasp are new perfumes, reverberating as the music does, down through time. She leaves the piano and unpages her white blouse and walks out of that entitled wrapper illustrated by scent; her smile reaches down her front and widens her skirts like meadows with a secret stream running through their folds. Having once played, the pianism is present in every letter of any treatise that was present. Now return the bland and snot-spotted library books quickly, and hope the librarian will not cotton on that we have taken back musical boxes.

Second Day

This is a dream she had on the second day of her menstrual bleeding. She was trampling the grapes in a wooden vat with her partner. He held in his hand a sample secret of his strength, the vine, with its great bunches of grapes. That same strength was being trampled underfoot. What was his name? His proper names were originally cries; 'Iacchos' was a song. A spurt of juice drenched her garment; now Aphrodite was born from the purple foam. The stained garment flowed down like a shining nakedness. Out of a girl he created the goddess around whose body desire and rapture flowed in the guise of wet clothing. A presence was created by this act, *parousia*, the second coming. This was in the domain where all flows, which is sketched in her wine-drenched dress from which the bouquet of the vintage blazed with the sound of trumpets. He was the Lord of all that is wet and shining. The bouquet in which she stood was a twining flame so purple that it was invisible. It was sounding as a trumpet sounds, but both above and below the limit of audibility. This was their intercourse today; there was no other touch and this was total touch. She cried to wake, and the vintage flows on to her sheets.

The Oracle Again

The oracle taken by casting Guinness on a white shirt. This portly expanse of linen, its buttons pouting, curvaceous over the universal belly-frame – on its taut crossings of threads, the warp and woof of forces that alter us all, million-graticule garment registering in cobweb-stirrings posture, breath, and all matters that alter under the weather, comprehensive dial-and-pointer – Oh, excuse me, Sir, I was carrying out a universal experiment – regard the balance and distribution of this hurtling fluid; as it halts suddenly it paints the shape of all the forces acting on it and upon your flesh and upon your shirt at this dynamite instant, and no offence intended. (But if that last part were true, why then did I choose the ugliest man in the room on whom to demonstrate my action-oracle, that the paw-mark of God would be revealed?).

Annual Event

Pamela, in a green dress, came and sat down in the water, to show us. We blessed her for it, and applauded heartily. I found the hotel at last, in which the conference was being held, the solid and staid old Edwardian, the Metropole. Discreet notices printed in a whisper found me the great ballroom. Bowls of water were brought in, and the delegates, removing trousers and knickers, sat down in the bowls in a silence of profound concentration. It was cold water, with ice-cubes. Then bowls of warm water were brought in, substituting for the others. I counted eighty delegates. It was the annual pile-shrinking competition.

Mudlark Instructions

A person whose lights are not lit may acquire an ambiguous phosphorescence by rolling in mud. Approach the sludge lagoons at dusk through silver birch, your heart in your mouth, your clean clothes rustling. Teeter on the turf brink facing the array of calm black mirrors which are directed at the sky to absorb all rays from the cosmos and to precipitate them as itself, for that is why they are black. Had you microscope-equipment you would understand that you are standing in front of a great laboratory lying on its back. This laboratory throngs with the ghosts of trees, which are being treated with both electricity and perfume by an indigenous workforce. You are about to become that laboratory. But feel the tension between cloud and lake, head and soles; fear and longing renders you an instrument suitable to take its place in the halls of process and becoming, which are made of glass-grains and water as well as ghosts so green they are black and the halva of germs. Now you are ready. Close the knife-switch! Fling yourself full-length through the mirror; join yourself with your shadow!

After a while, roll on your back and observe that the stars have come out in the black mirror of the sky. But are you in the sky, hovering over the earth of stars, or are you earth upon earth, as it were contained in the black bowl of a radio-telescope? Are you fouled, and dreaming of cleanliness; or immaculate and deserving maculation? Out of a cloudless sky a little clean rain begins to fall.

Greedy Green

Then I was living in a shop-front. Everybody could see all my details as they passed, the High Street crowds knew me, they stared with one stare from a million eyes. But in the cardboard and matchboard show-bathroom I drew real water from the taps, and the stare grew more intense, and brought its feet hurrying to the window. This tapwater was however green, and I was drawing a green and scummy bath for myself. How could I get clean in that water? So, rolling up my sleeve to fish around for the plug I discovered I was naked. The stare was amused at my evident consternation. I would not get in that bath at any price, skin or no. I plunged my arm in the water and found something sodden and silky there, and I pulled out of the veridian fluid the corpse of a small bird. I was aware that the High Street stare was craning over my shoulder. I spun round and threw the bird at them. They recoiled, and I could hear through the glass their collective intake of breath. The bird stuck on the glass, then slid down leaving feathers behind, stuck in its putrid track. I heard a soft detonation from the bath, and another swollen and bedraggled corpse bumped to the surface. At that point the woman woke me by making love, but I saw cruelty and greediness in her High Street stare like viridian rain.

Gentle Places

The rider opened his coat and showed like a ball of fire. He asked Billy mildly what he had done with the money, showing like an autumn fire riding a horse all the time. His skull was the whirling smoke on its long neck. The horse grazed with tranquility during the fire's utterances. All this occurred by the field where the archbishop was beheaded. Billy told; the ghost had done its work, it was last seen in quite a different mood: following Billy's corpse at the funeral and, at midnight, smoke grey, gliding away over the ploughed fields towards the graveyard, where it sang a second service for that vicious thief. The ghost now had a taste for our earth and, to quench his fire, haunted shit-houses. It was fine to hear Mr Cornish tell him he was in hell. They laid him with gravel in a pit for fifty years. Some are only bound with sand, but they generally work free and have to be bound with bricks. At the back of High Peak and between there and Peak Hill is a bad place – we call it a gentle place. It is a flypaper for such ghosts as venture near. You must beware of the trees planted in such places. The ghosts achieve utterance in their wind-blown leaves and tell only their nightmares day and night, never their true stories.

Partying in the Rain

I. *Chinese Flesh, English Skeleton*

The Chinese woman's face was severely pock marked, like a
yellow moon. She wore a black silk long dress, and a ruby ring
on her forefinger. She liked cheese. She had grown up in
Birmingham, where she had been a hairdresser. After years of
hard work, she ended up owning three shops. She had sold
them and moved down south. She said it was because of the
Thames, which she loved. Body-language of different people,
the smell of their clothes because of a different diet; I did not
know or care whether she was Chinese or not; she did not
smell Chinese, though the face was an important aspect of the
edifice of course, but was our whole body not replaced every
seven years? Topped up with Birmingham bone and blood?
Chinese flesh, and English skeleton. She had a sinewy intensity.
Caught in the rain at our party her dress shone like a black
mirror; afterwards she had stripped without selfconsciousness;
but she would not put on the clean jeans I offered her from
the airing cupboard. 'Can I wear that?' she pointed to a dark-
brown sheet, and arranged it about her in the manner of a
sari. She grew animated in her Midlands voice when we were
talking about the ordination of women, and told us how she
had seen on television the women in the Synod's public bal-
cony weeping as the motion was refused. 'Pique' – Simon
was cleaning the rust off an old Chinese dagger. I wondered
whether this meant he would like to sleep with the Birmingham woman. 'No,' she said, 'the women were weeping because
they knew what they had to give, and were not allowed to
give.' Is this Chinese? I think so. I wanted to sleep with her.
The first time that I met her, her breath smelt of apples, something stamped with the stars: I mean the five pointed star at
the fruit's core. Her collar was open just to the breastbone
point, where the indrawn breath exactly balances with the
exhalation.

II. *A Small Ventriloquism*

She, or he, has dragged a rustic table out of the shed. She has laid the big drawing-board across it so that gives an even surface. On this surface she spreads a green cloth. She produces out of pockets a number of things. A penknife, which she opens, and lays down. A small dish as an ashtray in which she places her cigarette-holder, and an earthenware cup, out of which she has been drinking vodka. Now she perches on the stool, and looks at us and grins. We rustle uncomfortably, in our party clothes. Bo – she says suddenly, pushing her face forward. In my mind I see a snake; it is her green outfit, which matches her eyes. A splash of rain on my hand. Well, the entertainment, whatever it is, will have to continue indoors. In a minute it is pouring, but we do not wish to move. We realise that the tension that has dogged us all afternoon and made the party a failure is coming to its consummation in this rain, and fading away. It was undoubtedly this which sent her out to make her little booth. Now she shines in the rain like some Robin Hood indifferent to the weather, the feather of her hat striking straight up into the dazzle. We suddenly realise how wet we are, and begin to gather our soaking selves up, our cottons turned to fine heavy silks in the rain. As we crowd the bathrooms and bedrooms to dry and change, there is a wonderful smell of rain and greenery, as though the house was also a portion of outdoors. Relaxing in our dry clothes it is as though the walls are alive, and the air between us and them charged with elasticity, the partitioned vessels of air which are the rooms acting as some kind of complex vessel in which distillations are occurring, ourselves both distillers and what is distilled. Our entertainer is the last to take her bath. I finish putting my lipstick on in the mirror. Reclining in the bath fully clothed she remarks: 'Don't blame me for the rain. I was only going to do a small ventriloquism,' and she pointed to the soaked fairy-doll that sat perched on her feet up at the tap-end. 'Merry Easter' called the doll, waving her diamond-tipped wand.

Hamlet

In the pub a woman suddenly dashes a pint of Guinness over her own white and frilly-bloused front. Hamlet, who has experience in talking to ghosts, is amazed. Is this a fetish, or a ghost-exercise? The latter, I think: notice that her eyes are closed. It is an event that might more readily occur in a dream, some deluge of the spiritually alert body, both desired and feared, ghost-shaped. Now she is savouring the sensations. In a moment she will open her eyes and inspect the copious external stains which splash and spread in the pattern-resultant of all the forces in the universe dwelling in that blouse at this moment of impact. Later she will discuss the matter with her male partner, who is at the moment giving her action room, as he is frozen in astonishment. Meanwhile the complex clean-ironed cotton recording-instrument sensitive to vectors inner and outer that go to make up its display, the draught from the swing-doors, the thumping of her heart, the field of electro-magnetism held in the crosswork of silky threads, transforms in an instant to a time-warp printout of these local and universal influences – something for dwarfish time-bandits to steal off her back. Moreover, the presence or utterances of ghosts can affect the wordage of this giant stain, which is also an emblem, a bringing out into the open of her menstruation, which this act has just started. The mantic or divinatory characteristics are identical to the ink splashes, sand-trays, tea-leaves, sfumage, écremage, decalcomania and powdering of clairvoyants and surrealists. In addition the magnificent nose of the ferment arises around us all black as the Guinness itself, but invisible, and as powerful an aid to the genius as years of scripture itself read aloud out of Guinness-coloured books to boys in dusky churches in which their white surplices seem to glide in procession like foam down a gullet.

Now this pint has been laid out by this lady, it is a flat pint, like a sliced tree-trunk showing its rings over which balsamic sap creeps, except for its perfume, which swells in all perceptible dimensions through the room, warmed by her chest and by our astonishment. She has extracted the bouquet, using the laboratory of her gifted chest, now dark as Sheba's. Guinness got laid; it is a fast partner; and love-smells fill the bar. Now she strips the blouse off, shakes it, cracking it like a whip, and hangs it out to dry on a neighbouring chair-back. 'I'm sure Bobby's coming after all,' she says to her companion, and takes out her purse, goes up to the bar in her bra and orders another round. She is served without question. Her companion repositions the chair nearer the radiator, so the blouse will dry faster. It is Hamlet himself who acts thus considerately, who happened to be sitting with this woman who understands fluids and their transformative use a degree better than poor Ophelia with her unfermented posies. As the lady returns to her seat, Hamlet leads a round of applause among the habitués. 'That's the way to talk to ghosts, all right,' says Hamlet, who also enjoys dressing in white and black. Meanwhile, the pattern on the steaming blouse begins to sketch a Veronica resembling Hamlet's Father's beetle-browed face – contracted there more in sorrow than in anger.

Two Tales of Hoffmann

I.

'Serpent? The moon sloughing light over the trembling water, the female orgasm, what you will!'
'That's not nice, Olympia. You should not refer so directly to your snake.'
'My cunt, father.'
The doll on the old man's knee was dressed like a Miss Faversham, in a cobwebby wedding dress. The lipstick on her wooden face was smeared, and since she was a doll, this was like a dissolution of her substance rather than a displacement of cosmetic. They sat in the inglenook of the Seven Stars; I and the barman were the only other ones there. I was pleased to see them, as I was looking around for old men to get on with. My father had recently died, and I needed to talk to men of his age, to make reparations; my grief attacked me with a sharper tooth because I had not got on with him. I heard the two voices in the inglenook before I saw them. Helplessly I dropped down on the facing seat.
'I like young men,' said the doll. 'I hope you're not a poet. It was a poet busted my spring.'
'Nonsense, my dear,' soothed the old man, and moved a hand in the interior of her back. There was a whirring noise, and her full skirts blew out all around her, like Marilyn Monroe standing over the grating. I leaned across and touched the little hand in its white glove. Was there a midget in that soiled dress? The hand was warm, and I was gripped firmly in my turn.
'Is it real?' I whispered.
'I'm not an it,' said the little shrill voice. I was watching the old man's lips, but they only twisted in a tight smile. I could not see that he made the voice. He held the doll out at me.
'Be like the poet,' he said, 'bust a doll. Chuck it in the fire.

It's only cloth and cardboard. Go on – oh I'll do it for you since you won't do it for yourself!'

With a quick movement he flipped his wedding-doll into the big warm fire. Immediately it became a scrabbling kind of a blind animal and a steam went up out of it and it shrieked.

'That is the air coming out of its bellows,' said the old man, calmly.

Now it had uplifted arms of flame in sleeves of flame. I found myself standing up and reaching into the fire.

'Don't be an ass, man,' the old man said as I tried to get hold of the log that was burning on top of the glowing coals, a fresh sappy green log that spat, hissed and covered itself with steam.

'I think you must have fallen asleep for a bit.' Under his white fringe of hair his wrinkled face was kinder and more considering than I had thought.

'The fire's warmth is almost hypnotic...' I nodded my head dumbly.

He started laughing then. 'It's worse if you're a poet,' he cackled.

II.

Hoffmann knocked at the laboratory door in the back lane. He was in search of old men who would impart their secrets. The lock clicked and the door swung open. A little old man with a fringe of white hair, bent into the automatic courtesy of old people, bowed him in through heavy draft-excluding drapes. As the old man lifted the curtains, Hoffmann was conscious of a wonderful smell. He snuffed it up with evident pleasure, stepping into it as though to get more. He turned to see the old man watching him with a smile.

'It's jasmine, isn't it?' asked Hoffmann.

'Not exactly,' replied Coppelius, 'it's electricity. Without the electrical field the flowers would smell as they commonly do; it is these the smell comes from.' They passed into the hall, where a dark table held a bowl of bright yellow flowers. 'Buttercups!' said Hoffmann, 'normally they smell hardly at all.' 'Would you like to go directly upstairs? While the electrical field is switched on, you will hardly know her. But she tells me she has been waiting for you for a long time.'

The English Yogi

I.

This field of harvest is a feathering wing. I see the whole of harvest Britain as a flying pastoral island. It is this field that makes – how many English muffins? I have always wanted to try the tablecloth experiment on a really large table. Whisst! I have snatched the broad field of linen from under the undisturbed silver places, which shine reflected in the dark wood like the constellation 'Dinner'. I have broken one crock which lies shattered, the butter oozing out of the English muffins. We see all this by the cascading light of the electric chandelier; and I see too your anger with a small dark flexible man. But look! I can twist myself so that my head as normal is smiling and twinkling at you from between my upstretched legs as I balance on the points of my buttocks. Is that not fine?

II.

The bedrock beneath meadow, hill and parkland is great stone mirrors onto whose face harvest electricity has oozed from above and etched its eternal patterns through millenia of crops. I can see this by my meditation balanced on my buttocks, while the English butter soaks into the carpet. These lightless stone mirrors shine to my third eye as brilliantly as the upper wheat, these great harvests of stone radio, the underworld of Pluto, God of Riches. You can hear the underwheat hiss on your transistor, between stations. Grind your wheat and bake your bread right and it will take an impress from the electromagnetism below, the one above will correspond to that below, and you will get electrical bread. The churches know the secret. The pictures of all weathers are stored there too, and accumulate by formative causation or habit, so after one dry hot summer you are likely to get another by subterranean reinforcement, and the cloudbursts in February accumulate emphasis by repetition. Such regularities become tyrannous. You can break them by making love with me in this egregious posture – come, I have spoilt our English tea-party, a suitable interval has passed since luncheon, let me teach you limb-writhing on an empty stomach.

III.

I am known by a woman's name, since women are able to see into the land and its bedrock mirrors with the aid of their mirror of blood. I do not have a womb, unlike you, Lady Rose, but I polish the inside of my skin by breathing in a certain way so that it is like a dusky one-way mirror, and, when I close my eyes, is perfectly transparent from where I live (though you may glimpse in it distorted images of yourself, and this makes you passionate). It is in this manner that I watch electrical matters as I please, and their landscapes, impalpable, odourless, silent and invisible to the rest of you, form themselves to me as fascinating palaces in the centre of which I sit on the points of my buttocks, in contemplation. This is another reason for the woman's name: I have exchanged doing for being, and I carry my own electrical palace around with me which, if you could see it, would resemble a woman's flowing ballgown.

IV.

Others are so clothed, and from time to time in these palaces I open a door with mental force and find behind it a glittering ball in progress, and I join the dancers for a spell. On other occasions a spirit greater by far passes in front of my face and my hair stands on end over my entire skin, and I become like an untouchable hedgehog, or a cloud pouring out its thin lines of rain. However, the yogi contemplating sky-images with eyes closed and skin open can sometimes as in a magic lantern project some personal pattern of his choosing over the entire sky. A slight effort of projection, and the cumulus breaks up and reforms in the letters 'To the Lord of Yoga – Salutations from this World,' then a map of Falmouth forms in the sky for the use of visitors and after that lightning strikes the hills over by Flushing. The women are amazed and pleased, the men look angry, and tap their riding-crops against their booted thighs.

V.

As a woman can satisfy more than the one man, as a woman can reach into herself and find sexual resources without apparent limit, so this yogi has learned an identical lesson and I can therefore with my penis of moderate Dravidian proportions erect a great staircase of tumescence up which I accompany my many partners arm in arm and leg in leg negotiating in prolonged ecstasy the plushy stairs made of both of us. No, Lady Rose, it is too late – I have already sent out the invitations in your name to the party-game called 'Crossing the River' in which every lady will be arranged recumbent by title along the Long Gallery, and then under the old masters and family portraits I will satisfy turn by turn an aggregate of six thousand years of English history (allowing half a millenium per distinguished title) and British female aristocracy in the persons of these matriarchs, beginning at one end of the gallery and slipping out afterwards by the small wooden stair at the North end to my bath and shower.

VI.

Now this room is renamed the Haunted Gallery and its visitants are sweet smells and puffs of incense, glad singing cries and naked images of a yogi and yoginis in conjunction in the shoulder-high electrical ripening wheat rooted in the subterranean temples that produces its characteristic tingle of wellbeing in the whole skin, for nobody can view this visitation without participating; and, moreover, this gallery is Glorious because I have pleasured the family ghosts too, and this above all renders the land fertile and the skies bright.

Dance the Putrefact

Scenario for a Masque

'As he lay on his back, stretched out on the ground, with arms extended, he marked himself out with stones – the shape of his body, head, legs, arms, and everything. There you can see those rocks today. '

Old Man Creates – *The Hero with a Thousand Faces:* JOSEPH CAMPBELL

I.

'The Avenue of the Giants,' he said calmly. Meaning the trees, introducing me to the Village. I have come here because I have a dance. All here have come for similar reasons. Here nobody pries or condemns. Your dance is not mocked, since mockery distorts the dance. Everybody here has been dance-blind, and here some have recovered their sight.

II.

We were walking in the woods near the Falling Leaf Tavern, with its cellars full of liquor made in autumn. We had explored the avenue of great trees tossing their heads, with the church at the far end whose font was full of the surprising water. The dance of dust over the surface of the holy water in the font made visible the constant movement in the consecrated water. We had seen above the village the flat dancing-ground that had never been touched by a shod foot. I removed my shoes and socks and walked with my companion on to the hard flat ground dustless and warm. From this platform we surveyed the village. Tall columns of bonfire-smoke climbed into the still air, spiralling and twining from the villagers' gardens. We had descended and walked along the tidal inlet towards the beaches. The tide was low and we strolled by flat sheets of black mud, watery earth, earthy water. Secretly in my mind I hear the first steps of my dance. Warm fires glow from the windows as we return in the twilight. We pass a smouldering bonfire deep within which, as in a cage, mice of fire still race.

III.

Smelling of new-baked bread and sawdust in the early sun, glossy as chocolate, soft as drifted flowers, the floor of my dance is prepared by the salt tide. I hear the great mud-drum Its first beat ripples to the farthest shore. It is a liquid mattress, a slack trampoline, cradle and grave.

IV.

I am very strict, in order that I may be very grotesque. I am very strict, because I am very grotesque. My white shirt is without spot, its collar-lappets ironed smoothly back, a red scarf tucked in the opening. My trousers of an equivalent whiteness, demarcated by a broad dark belt. Like a cricketer I am white, like a morris dancer I carry a withy, a willow wand. I am a person of sheer whiteness save for a slice at the waist, standing at the brink of capacious black. With my feet bare I advance towards the soft black mirror.

V.

With the strokes of my withy and my bare footprints I dance my reflection on the mud. The mud is firm but quaking, soft as a strewing of dark flowers over a firm beachsand. This is the way I dance my figure. Leaning out over the mud, with my long withy-wand I draw stretching out as far as I can two crescents, their bulge towards me. They are the eyebrows. With a cry I leap over them and land up to my ankles. These prints are the socketed eyes. With a sliding step I slive out the nose and stand working the trench of the long mouth a pace away. With my wand I enclose these features in a head. I pass on to the throat and stroll out a left arm, a right arm – the hands come later – with a second bound I am ankle deep in two nipples, whose breasts I now scribe from my vantage points. A third hop, legs clapped together, gives me the navel, from which, swivelling, I mark out chest-lines and transverse ribmarks. Down the midriff I dance the long cunt, I furrow, I delve, I dance its extent many times, it splashes me, I am dark to my belt. I dance along the waist and make a left leg, returning to the cunt. I dance a right leg, returning to the cunt. I finish off the arms with hands that grasp and spread the cunt. I take a fourth leap, and am standing in the feet of my creature. I face the sun over the sea, she streams behind me like my shadow, the small clear wavelets advance towards me over the tidal mud. I turn, I pluck my feet out and stamp them down facing my creature, my left foot in her right, her left foot accepting my right. The sun behind me from the east casts my shadow into her outlines and she configures with this part of me. It is time to give myself up to the dance.

VI.

I am down, and within her! I have vaulted into her boundaries and I am as black as she is. I am buried deep in her flesh. I pull her flesh off her in handfuls and cover my skin in hers. I prance, cool and nightladen with exterior cunt. The black bed before me is rucked. The black woman-outline has risen from it and I dance within her skin. I am the black woman. I am petal-soft, and my surfaces are rounded and shining. The bosom of my shirt is heavy with mud. It hangs and flounces like large breasts full of black milk. The black lady minces sadly loverless over the mud, she smells of tar and sunlight. Where is this white lover? She dances sadly on her own. Soon her lover will return, but her disappearance is the condition of his return. She will enjoy the sunlight while she can. Soon her ladyhood will pour like black blood through the drains of his bathroom, she will fade like a shadow in a shower of clear water.

VII.

Why do I return again and again to this same action? Because it is my dance. No one here gives reasons or asks questions. We are here in this village in order to dance. His dance is all a person has. It is his datum. But I, I cannot read my dance, and until I can do so I am condemned to enact it, and am imprisoned within it. I am dance-blind. There are so many other dances I could join! But now the season approaches in which all the dances are joined into one, the time when all the people's dances are performed together. For the first time in my life I shall perform my dance among all the others, with others watching. None will blame and none will condemn, for each person has his dance. This season approaches.

VIII.

That season arrived this morning with the blowing of trumpets! Six men in Sunday black clothes wind the silver trumpets. Six women in village white bow the small dark violins. The music awoke me in my great tavern bed. I gather up my dancing-clothes, which have been cleaned and ironed for me without comment. I dress quickly and carrying my wand I clatter down the wooden stairs. Outside I join the procession of people dancing to the music up the hill to the smooth stamped platform. The Flora Dance plays from the six loudspeakers on poles that line the route. The sun shines. I hear the Flora Dance play through the innumerable beaks of all the birds.

IX.

I am afraid. How can I dance my desire on this hard earth? I have watched the others dance the dance of their own lives, the dance they wished to read. The music falls silent and they dance to the sound of their own flesh. There is a lady presenter with a forked twig who touches the heads of those who are to dance. I have watched the man who dances the tearing and devouring of human flesh; companions are selected by the lady to dance the dismemberment he wishes. They jerk and thrash on the dancing-ground like farmyard carcasses; he stuffs his mouth with the pink flesh greedily; the soaking of blood into the ground is danced with wriggling fingers. What if I were selected to dance this part by the lady? Would I do the dance justice, imprisoned in my own? I have watched three men dance the fuelling of ovens with their fellow-dancers. I have watched the old woman who dances the sewing of clothes over and over. Certain partners dance their assemblage into great costly garments as she stitches their bodies together; at last she rends them and the bodies scatter. She dances only with her rags. I watch a great company of men and women who dance a Parliament, and I watch the enacting of just and unjust laws, I see the Parliament dance its sinking into the ground, not a stone left on stone, and a new assembly arises. I watch a household dance the knocking together of a ship of great size from the bodies of other dancers, from which they exclude a certain company. However, certain dancers dance animals, who are admitted, and the remainder dance drowning, crying silently and clinging to the ark's human timbers as it sails without them. The lady presenter touches with her twig the heads of those who are to dance drowning. She does not touch my head with her invitation, even for that.

X.

The lady passes among the dancers and signifies the beginning or the end of their dances; she turns them out of their courses with the touch of her twig. She is dressed in spotless white, more plainly than a bride, in a manner suitable for dancing. Her feet are bare, her skirt is pleated, she is fair-haired. She must be the chief dancer, since the others obey her, and obey the language of her wand. Now as chief dancer she begins to dance the flowers turning to the sun and the tides turning to the moon, the chief dance that lies within the others. She dances alone, the men watch her from an outer ring that surrounds the dancing-ground, she is watchful among them for a partner. She touches certain of the men with impatient strokes of her twig, and they join her in the centre. The men line up in a row, crouching, with their backs to her. The lady wanders behind them, inspecting, pausing as if to choose, rejecting, passing on, lingering on some detail of their dancing clothes, touching lightly the brim of a hat, a frayed cuff, the sailor-collar of a shirt, the bare nape of a neck, a chain around the neck, seeking, passing along the line, turning on her heel, returning.

XI.

She has chosen her dancer and they dance joy! There is a sigh from all the company. She has stopped behind one man. She has thrown her wand away from her high over the heads of the spectators. She steps close in to him from behind and crouching like him rests her elbows on his shoulders, her wrists turned to the front. Her thumb-joints lie with gentle pressure on his temples and her fingers stretch out to suppose horns on his head, eight-tined horns. He is chosen as stag, and the lady will ride him, 'and tempt him, and he will ride the lady. There is a dance of riding and intercourse led by the lady and the man. They dance on their heels to signify the possession of hooves. There is charging and division, there is stamping and calling, there is rolling, there is slow beating with the feet until the ground and the hills rumble and the hills to me sitting in the shade, no member of the dance, the hills begin to slide. There is conjunction and division, there is breathing and sweat, there is the thumping of bare feet, there is the occasional cry as the dancers turn but no further song. There is a serpentine dance that coils figures of eight between the lady and her stag who stand making two centres slowly turning to watch each other over the heads of the winding people. I who have not been chosen cower for fear lest I intercept the glance of one or the other.

XII.

Now the procession reforms and to the sound of the trumpets and violins which replace the body sounds that were the only dancing-music, the villagers descend to their houses. None of them looks at me. I fall in at the tail of the winding procession when I have seen that they wish to pass me by. The procession dances a slow step in triple time to the music. My feet drag along the grassy path. I expect the procession to disperse in the village square. I turn into my doorway but my arms are gripped. With serious faces the two hinder dancers force me to continue with them, for the column of dancing figures has not dispersed after all. As we approach the tidal mud-flats, the musicians fall silent again, and the only sound is the chafing of skin across earth.

XIII.

The tides have left my dancing-floor glossy and unmarked. The people assemble on the bank, they pass me forward, and sign to me that I must begin my dance. I lean forward and trace the first features of my shadow-figure. I bound off the bank and stamp eyes. My fear has gone. With lively steps I leap and prance until I stand in the feet of my completed figure, facing out to sea, the red sun at my back. I turn and pluck my feet out and stamp them down facing the throng. They are black figures on the red sunlight sending long shadows down into the mud. Suddenly one leaps out of the sun into the mud and stands thigh-deep in the thighs of my figure. She is in white. Her forked stick stays planted deep in the soft bank, a thrumming silhouette. She crouches and draws herself knees to elbows into the trench of the black cunt. She rolls round deepening the hole and covering herself with black likeness. She flings her arms and legs wide inside the figure in a black star like a navel.

XIV.

I caper with my black lady in the mud. Both lovers are present at the same time, at last. I dance earth and water. The sun dances fire. It reddens the black mud. I am a seed in her red flesh, she pulls me out of the red mud, we are trees laden with red leaves, we are glistening red serpents slithering in the mud. We dance seamless blood-marble with our sour-sweet skins joined. We interchange our red shining skins by scooping

c

and plastering. We fashion new and surprising organs and wear them proudly for a while and then dash them away. She grows a mud-baby under her flounced and clinging skirt, and I suckle our baby with red milk out of the bosom of my shirt. We bury our baby and we stamp until it dissolves, until its very memory dissolves, then we resurrect our child. I bury her and she buries me in our world bed and we make red love in the queasy bed until the ripples of our embrace reach the farthest shore. Who are these people who signal the end of our dance with silver trumpets, with small dark violins tucked under the chins? We rise, and tear off our garments and trample them in the mud underfoot. We dance towards the crisp foam that dances towards us as the tide rises. My red lady enters the white foam, I enter, the trumpets sing from their silver throats all around us.

XV.

I run gasping from the foam. The people advance to meet me and to the sound of trumpets and violins clasp a garment about me to warm my body. I turn impatiently from them to where my lady should rise from the sea to join me. The sea is empty and the foam crisps gently in hollow waves. The people draw me sobbing and shivering away from the sea and its empty foam.

XVI.

This lady has ended in the sea, just like the lady I made for myself. This dance is no better than the other! The dancers dry my tears and urge me with many gestures to join in their dance. Why should I dance with people who are no more than foam and mud and tears dancing on empty bones! But as I dance loverless, I forget. Another lady steps into the circle and dances to help me remember.

XVII.

Our dance ended at the tavern door, we have climbed the wooden stairs, this new lady and I, we have bathed, and slept in the great bed, and we are dressing each other. I button her blouse gently close up to the neck so that the points of her collar make a little A. I pass her pendant engraved with the A and the V inside the 0, over her fine dark hair. She buttons my shirt but leaves it open so that my throat is bare in a V. The sun and the moon circle without end over and under our bed and our table. The rain beats on the hard-packed dancing-ground, and beyond it the sun sets into tango fire like a launching-pad. The moon beats out her triple-time. The clouds draw out of the waves and fall foaming, and shed their peacock rainbows as they will. The moon is an endless necklace of white ladies, red ladies, black ladies always leaving, always returning. I fasten her necklace loosely around her collar. The blood beats time in our warm throats.

❦ II.
DR LUCKY

A Crystal of Industrial Time

I.

The entering of her was like eating a little spoonful of golden syrup warmed over a candle-flame. Her cunt gave off a round heat that was in itself a dream. There was instant hypnosis, and an immense river-bridge between us that was slowly and inexorably vibrating. Much traffic passed across that bridge which as the trance darkened began to blaze with lights. The refrigeration of a lorry had broken down and the drivers had stopped and opened it up and were giving away boxes of loganberries that would otherwise have spoilt. The fruit was warm as if it had just been picked. The soft fruit began to grow; it hung and twined about the bridge creating gardens, and the traffic gratefully collecting syrups turned into every insect in the world comprising a portrait in the making and still wet in sliding oils and hard carapaces and painted wings of a single personage not yet named. It was that person, whether deity or animal, who slept. Waking, two bodies were very clearly discernible; and of that third person I could trace nothing but a faint perfume, the one who had been bridge, lorries of loganberries, and hanging garden.

II.

Dreams inspired by the sound of falling water, the bells covered in singing birds, vast eyelids of mirror. Now the child and the machine meet. The great cogwheel taller than a man propped on the wharf; the daughter stopped in her tracks regarding this magic circle standing up of itself: is it a star, a pathway, a knot, a garden? She glances aside, at the clouds among the trees of small rain walking the pavingstones. No, this is the skeleton of a powerhouse, the bones of rigid circular force, it spins so fast it looks silky or may pace in jerks, jig, jag, counting its flow into compartments. This nocked wheel does not exist within nature, unless something like it, painted black, cogs the stars, and a piece has fallen. It is a crystal of industrial time. She is a sprite, matter raised to human grace; it is a child of the mines, a mother-substance turned into the image of sixty-fold click clack, it ends nowhere and begins here: not begins, *meshes*. She arrives at Sunday, and dances on to the cog dropped from God's black watch. Is it a star, a pathway, a knotgarden? It has engaged her, it is the skeleton digit of a powerhouse, the third on the left hand, it is the transmitter of rigid circular force, all its days are identical, day and night; it is the opposite of rain, mother's breast, pouring waterfall.

III.

The weather plays with my age. Here comes an old Lear-like cloud with a terrific flowing beard and the look of somebody who is very grey and very much wrinkled but who is going to shout at the top of his voice, and I noticed him arrive because I became suddenly bad-tempered here down below and irascible words entered my mind as simply as handmaidens – then I looked up and saw that this floating personage was about to force me into his invisible replica mask of electrical bad temper. Now here comes the sunny sky moving in ragged casements of sunshine sliding over the country and my wrinkled mask snaps off and I smile with the sunshine and words surround me with a Sunnyjim glow and I can bless and receive blessings among which is the elixir of youth, and this is because these heavy clouds carry ten years in their luggage which they drop over you; but then the rain falls and you can run and laugh through the puddles and somehow ten years are lost and washed away; but, beware, the aches and pains which were galvanism of the sky falling down all around are now rheumatism and the encroaching beards of death; the thunder sounds and his heart stops, and no amount of sunshine will start it again.

IV.

Each droplet of the fog a globe of perfume, a small crystal bottle of the cloud that has been gathering odours over the whole mountain. Here comes the cloud with its pillars and porticos, its studies and its jails. It is a perfumer's shop-cloud, it surrounds me with its samples breaking over my shoulders, it is gathering an essence from me also, and imparting one. I swear I can distinguish the owner and her assistants inside the cloud, bending over the array of phials, with tendril fingers of wind adjusting the display, picking a different scent from each atom.

V.

She says: one book opens another; one perfume reverberates another. The beauty of her geranium essence made me feel like a superb creature. I shook hands with him at the supermarket and it lasted me a week. In the Souk of perfumes we have a friend already. Having bought him patchouli I could detect a vertical rainbow based on the whole town, with its rearing ground-base of two or three square miles. As for burials: if we packed them into the sweet grass of the mountain limestone country, the dry grass will suck the liquors out of them and in return perfume the dry mummies light enough to be lifted between finger and thumb, like a woman-sized dry leaf that smiles upwards with its teeth and nails fastened in the date-hued skin. As for the woman's perfume we bought together: he has led me by its means into my secret wine-cellars.

VI.

In conversation with the rector they explained: The play of love in joy and sorrow is a wonderful secret word. He wondered if he agreed. They said: there is odor divino as the senses open. He was with them there. The holy rauch and the divine schmack. Those are unusual words but they carry their message, he agreed. The fragrance of God solidifies to become a cloud overshadowing the soul. Certainly Moses met God in the cloud and conversed with him. The Cloud was God's odour, rector, and we endlessly be all hyd in God...hym delectably smelling. I have heard that woman never left Eden. That's a bit stiff, said the rector to the lovers. The Song of Songs is so called because it is a doorway to the garden of spices which woman has never left, where she compiles her goods. What do you think about that, my dear, turning to her, do I smell God entering the room, or it is Eve alone, or among her wreathing temptations. It is by far the best thing that we should all remove our clothes. Please allow me to finish my cigar, and must I preach Christie bonus odour? The perfume of your breath if speaking holy words is God's breath; it is a sweet smell of oonheed, or unyoun which the devil cannot smell, and the murmuring touch in the mind's ear follows, for every knowyng of sothfastnes is a privey sownynge of Iesus in there of a clean soule. I hear you, says the rector. This is no after-dinner library of books, but Solomon's garden, for each book imparts its perfume to the breath as it is read aloud, if I read you aright, says the rector, for every perfume must speak or sing, for the dumb, blind odour without voice is the greatest of devils and one of the chief torments of hell, in any month of the year.

Excursions

'Quelle sorcière va se dresser sur le couchant blanc?'

I.

Like bunches of hairy flowers with eyes and teeth, prize dogs gathered by their leashes. Bag ladies picking up among the crowd. The beautiful soft green cloth tossed over the temper-steel safe. Easy, thou fool beast, easy...A grasshopper narrative: too much cold commotion.

II.

Talk flavoured by her full sleeves, words that would not have their savour without that dress. The women wreathed in their vapours, their invisibles. Her energy concentrated in the putter of her clothes over her neck restores the mind to its paradise of motioned rest, the fields and the woods fluttering at that throat; the cat in my chest leaped into those meadows and regions. I lay on the bed in the evening light and watched a speck of a moth land on the windowpane. It was the size of perhaps the half of a baby's fingernail, and on the pane it was lost in a vast area, like a single referee on the grass of an empty stadium. I could make out its caped shape as it walked. I saw that it was dressed in the long clothes of its wings, and this meant that I was visited as by a woman in a long dress, and her presence filled the room, even though I could see that its visible aspect was the speck of a moth the size of a grain of rye on a cloudy window. Its presence was of whatever size would fill the room, palace or home.

III.

The old man can do nothing. He nods his head as the bottle pops. The black bluebottle scrying at some invisible film on the dirty bar-top. The fly like the black cat, with head solid as a piece of coal and the limbs of a graceful waiter, wings like the skeleton of a leaf, his antennal procedures. She hugged the cat and shrunk him to her small and intensely potent body warmed with weak beer.

IV.

The end house at Jung terrace. The Alsatian jumped up at my hand. The tongue's coolness that touched me travelled right through that centre. I fall into the time of my pulse, or the dog's pulse. The warm-blooded maintain themselves in their own embrace, contain themselves in their own combustion; then there are the cool-blooded counsellors, the moth, the snake, the snowfall, the unheated blood that is open to every influence.

V.

The radiant throat the sign of the wedding of air and light. Seven lights burning on a great dark hull, as if the Great Bear had come to float in the river. And the 'Ghost Exercise': close your eyes and imagine that a fluid strikes you – then wait for further touches and whispers. All depends on this: I wear my pentacle ring on this finger because it is the womanly star, it is the applestar lodged on the clitoral finger which brings down star-jelly by maser: when I tickle you, you diffuse beneficent metals, the familiar room transformed by the sleeping body and its perfumes, wheat springing from her bodice of mud. When we touch our substance we stimulate the universe and ourselves simultaneously. All that glows sees. The horse we ride, the radiation between our legs. Beethoven flashing in my aura as I write. My father's ruby eyes flash. The last breath of the heir of the Roman father, the whole signature of the self in the astonished breath, as conscious and unconscious rush together in expiring death.

VI.

In September the male spiders run around sexually excited,
loping across our carpets and falling into the bath. The horned
owl moos, the thinking bird, the Moses bird. The woman
chalks upon the air with her emotions, she draws it deeply
into her lungs, splashing it out in great heated marks which
you can almost see. The little wood was called *Rupert's Copse*,
it was filled with cloud and it was sleepy; we rested on a gate
and could have slept there, sitting up like bones in a catacomb,
the wood joined up behind its own appearance into what one
could term a 'dream': the wood in the cloud. Entering it along
its broken paths was difficult and tiring, coming away from
it was easy, as though we had created corridors through the
heavy cloud spaces. A little rain came down upon her from
the branches. She wore a collar with nine points, as though
she had thrust her head through a blazing white star.

VII.

I had a sort of mutton-grey stubble and enormous lenses. We
smelt of rushes, and shivered too like rushes. I smelt of fur-
naces. In bed her desire seemed an apron of waterfall. This
sycamore is arrayed with perfumes which enter the world as
ideas and visions. There is a spirit seated everywhere; thunder calls forth its powers: Madonna Intelligenza, the health-
bearing understanding. A greyclad cloud of schoolboys: the
heads numerous as hail carried across counties by its cloud,
like castles of cobbles piling up in the reverse chasms. The
heads hail, the small voices thunder. The pleasure the tree
has in the water passing from tier to tier of its foliage like
shelves of metal. The animals blessing us in Egyptian. The cat
with folded paws and sistrum and a small pharoah carried
blessed on its forearm. The broad-shouldered, lion-headed
goddess with the pencil skirt. The goddesses seated in thrones
of three. The cat like a column of night; Anubis, the sharp
hound, staring at her with his ears; and the fully-human
goddesses stepping toward us no less regal than the sublime
animals.

VIII.

A half of whisky, a 'wee goldie', and the aurora flickering like firelight on the ceiling of the world. Sex was made sombre by her grey silk, and the pictures of child riders on all four bedroom walls. The flowchart of the world showed in the sky, it was light being ironed and folded and hung up and put on shelves. Her body-smoke was an aurora in the grey flue of her silk, I heard it rushing up through her collar. She dreamed of electricity, and a great electricity-station where the power was released merely by drilling in the earth. People danced in the excavation with coal dust smearing their grey silk. Her child came in and told us her dream: that the TV and the tumble-drier kept on turning on and working '...until I asked Mummy and she came and switched them off.'

IX.

The room was funky from the market of love. After despair there's nothing left but downpour. They move about in the grass in portable dome-shaped grass huts, demonstrating their invisibility to everyone. Lanterns bobbling in the wind like the captive souls of happy people. And then the black-masked cook removed their bones. The estuary under the glowering sky a deep silver grill full of foxfire flames.

X.

The Shakti wafts out after the instructions. The radiant bride called Niagra, in her sound and spray, in her white thunder. The whole county pithed with thunder. The wife one who would not be content with human men, only with the niagra-like operations of the Moon. She was bright, fiery, clever. Massaging the pussy-cat's neck she noticed not for the first time a certain note or feeling with an undertone to it like miscegenation, like love which was also a black poison, but in small doses under careful regulation a medicine.

XI.

I didn't push her into the mud! She called me from the earth, and I resisted her call. I pushed her away. She called me again and my eyes were multiplied. Thus I ate of the Tree of Knowledge, her hair spreading in the cloudy water like a huge weed.

XII.

The comets which blacked the ice cream; all production had to cease during the transit of the comet. The vast stainless Helmholtz lantern. The dumb-show of the production-line, the *mudras* and the *asanas* everlastingly repeated, the necessary attitudes of packing-schemata, the whole-cloud figures in white rubber boots, the visible breath, the array of cold piping, the vast stainless benches, the metal-doored hardening-room. The frosty path from the pasteuriser to the homogeniser. The snowmaiden icecream-makers. The damned great cold stores.

XIII.

The black mirror surrounding the body, the smoke stands still, the smoke of the black fire and there is a black flame standing round the body, a black mirror, ghost-in-the-flesh, the vapour full of images from all the plants; like that great perfume which rises from the open mines and links its arms over the whole of Cornwall, of the armamentarium of minerals, slowly grinding to grass and wheat; a human atmosphere which depicts the world motion, continual baptism made visible, the heart and the head bent humbly in its waves, the shirt expanding over the ribs like smoke, the puffed sleeves, the deep opening to the navel core from which the weather rises.

XIV.

The air blowing through her lungs, which are like the loose pink sleeves and neck of her light blouse, the buttons dropped like single notes of song down her front, the forest airs blowing through the sleeves and throat, the aurora of wood and candle-light, the ivy in showers of arrows shivering over the monuments, its shelves full of lambswool moths with tiger-eyes.

XV.

A wonderful smell of bitten apples came from the doctor as she completed her diagnosis. The skills she had. The skill of fabricating without lying. Of shouting to invoke her Goddess by punching a space in the air for her to enter. She rips open her shirt and hits herself in the face with her own prophetic vapour. It was the river that had flowed through her dreams. It was a river of hidden children, seeking to be born. The river of visions takes me as my lady opens her legs. No wonder they call it 'The Surgery'.

The Paradise of Storms

Salt and pepper stubble like little white crystals mixed with tiny black ones, aniline black with a silver halide, the skin planted with crystals like a landscape created by slow cooling, but really the stubble of a forest potentially, the hide creating around itself a swathing, for all changes. This crystalline scum expounding into a beard, the waves of beard flowing out of the skin ceaselessly, day and night, registering by a small agitation of growth as the trees do the presence of women and the growth-properties of the weather. Thus the beards, and the trees: this one knows that a woman waited under it an hour today during the rain; if we took a slice of its trunk and looked carefully at the fattening of the cambium which registers the shower, we would see a small figure with a closed umbrella. But that would be a barbarity, as they say of excessive beard-making. The tree-rings should be read without broaching the bark, by means of the perfume of which they are the emitting template, for the perfume of a tree compiles its experience as it matures. The great detective pauses under the tree in the garden of the murder-house and the name of the butcher passes into his mind like a whispering phantom which is the tree's perfume rising from every leaf. He lays his hand on the culprit's shoulder whose beard reeks bloody murder and an at-last-I-am-caught-and-can-rest blend of scents. Now the paradise of storms passes on, showing in every skin.

Confession

This morning began with opaque mists parting on very sunny rooms. It was not a day on which the earthquakes came out of their holes; it was too damp for that. Instead, somebody exclaimed in surprise at the figurative coiling of the ground mists 'The White Serpent!' Indeed as she pointed we could see that one cloud was marching with head high along the oak avenue before melting into the pond. Now it was as though the bright chambers of sunlight were speeding towards us. Now it was as if we had entered them and were carried along in brilliant gondolas through a writhing sea which sank away after a white deluge, leaving us soaked and confessed.

Dragon and Mistress

I went to change my book at the public library, which is in the Town Hall. I was chattering to myself about the unseemliness of a library, which should care for books, fining a person for reading one a second time. I had gone up those steps, muttering to myself, and through those doors a thousand times without looking at them, and that is how I found myself through the wound and inside the dragon before I realised it. I stopped and looked around me. The light had dimmed to a horny translucence. A blast of heat came rushing out of the reference library, or where it should have been, as if somebody had opened furnace-doors there. An ichor splashed down on my boot from the membraneous ceiling in a vivid brightness, which dulled. I poked at it with the point of my umbrella and it unstuck. I picked it up – it was a ragged plate of gold. I understood at last that I had arrived somewhere strange. I looked back the way I had come and saw the amber flesh closing down to a loophole. I sprinted out, bent double, and that was how I managed to save myself, though I dropped one of my books inside the dragon: *Light on Pranayama*.

A crowd was assembling out in the square. Two Woodrot Treatment vans were drawn up at the kerb. I knew from the local paper that this firm was to begin work today on longstanding dry rot in the Town Hall timbers, but their technicians stood there with all the other people, nonplussed, their equipment half-unloaded. We could not see the whole of the animal. It had coiled tightly round the building, so that the steps which normally led to a double-door entrance, now mounted to the great wound in its yellow-green and golden scaly haunch applied closely to the façade of the building. It was these steps I had run up absent-mindedly, clutching my books. The creature had coiled several times round the upper storeys and the final tail coil swished among the chimneys.

There was a fine incense in the air, like an autumn bonfire made with scented woods and spices, or a fire in a chemist's shop. The smell made a phrase float into my head: *High John the Conqueror Root.*

We could see that an enormous excavation had opened in the slate cliff behind the Town Hall, and this was where the remainder of the animal including the head must have been tucked. The visible coils on the front of the building clearly held the lungs, for they expanded and contracted very slowly from the steps to the second storey and back again, with the kind of deliberation with which the moon's shadow moves across the sun's disc during a solar eclipse. A great crack shot up the brickwork, and the windows burst from tne pressure of this breathing, as they did in the General Post Office next door; the ladies' loo on the other side was crumbling to pieces. I had escaped from inside the dragon just before exhalation closed the hot wound in the dragon's flesh; now inhalation was opening it again and you could see deep into the vaporous halls there.

The smell of spices was overwhelming, the crowd drew back. A bright ichor lolled out of the lower margin of the glowing wound and ran down the steps; I watched it cool, knowing it was molten gold. I could hear the leathery flesh creaking as the doorway expanded, but then another sound came hurtling towards us from the tall bow-bending incision. It was the shrieking of a woman. We could see her running towards us through the vapours, avoiding the molten puddles. She was at full stretch as she flung herself down the steps straight into my arms. Over her shoulder I saw the wound puckering as it contracted again in its cycle. The woman's dress was splashed with plates of gold which had charred the cloth and, cooling there, had stuck to it. She looked wonderful, splashed with that gold. Another phrase slid into my mind, *To gild the Queen sordidly.* Her eyes were slanting and green, and her body in my arms was taut and vibrant with her fear, and I felt a stirring of my own personal dragon. We began moving away through the crowd, which opened for us.

Now a squad-car with police drew up and a grand hooting heralded *les pompiers.* A fire-engine began pissing at the hot flesh of the visitant, creating swathes of steam behind which we could see the wound contracting painfully. This roused the dragon, brooding on the secrets of the cliff. Something like a small goldplaited royal coach began to drive slowly out of the dark excavation at the corner of the building. As the woman and I passed into the narrow streets of the town we saw that the dragon had pulled its great face up on its coils into the open air and was hovering it over the people. We did not linger. The mouth was fringed like a theatre-curtain, the big pale eyes were like floating mirrors. Were the people lingering in the square to be licked up by a fire-sticky tongue, or were they to be crushed in the Tiamat coils?

In the event the dragon vomited sicked-up gold in a sudden torrent like a collapsing Cinderella staircase out of the gaping mouth. Spectators were plastered upright where they stood, welded in golden chunks to the road. In the emergency measures which followed the encapsulated people were crow-barred off the street-surface and carried away like vast ingots in ambulances and carts. The dead were identified by casting plaster into the vacant moulds, which were then removed with goldsmiths' saws – for the hot metal vomit had vaporised the flesh beneath and calcined the bones to ash. The Government took the gold; the bereaved relatives were presented with the plaster statues. Most buried them in the normal fashion, though without coffins; a few younger people kept them around the house as remembrances, on the stairs, or propped up at the head of the dining-table or laid comfortably on a sofa.

As for the dragon, after upchucking, it flew away on thundering wings, though few had the leisure to observe it. It left behind in the excavation behind the ruins of the Town Hall a pile of auriferous waste from which all the gold had been smelted. The official theory was that the dragon was merely an electrical wind travelling in a chain of coherent vortices, and had been produced by excessive sunspot activity when the sun had risen in a part of the zodiac that had an affinity to the unworked seams of gold known to exist beneath Cornwall. There were new subsidences in certain mine-valleys, and these were pointed to, and the fact that there was nowhere any gold found in them was held to confirm the theory. It was the property of such wind to produce sensory distortions in the observers of it, which had led us in this case to believe we had been visited by a dragon – and the sudden earthing of its potentials by the hoses of the firemen had unloosed the hot ore carried in the plasma of the wind's belly, with much loss of life. But I say it was a dragon. How otherwise could it have carried to me a Chinese princess splashed with gold?

Everything They Tell Him Is True

I.

The forest jumping with particles of light distilled in water. The brook deep in the forest, one of the moon's ravelling sleeves. Cuff of moon, dark shirt of water. The forest by the sea, the docks among the tall senior trunks. Sun-thatched thunderclouds. Under the moon, the sea folding like fishskin. She builds her clothes up, the mirror about to shatter, the ceilings roaring with wind at dawn. Ice turning in its wide bed sky. A long mirror left in a forest, propped up against a beech. At the tip of every twig a distillate.

II.

The Sirens with their lodestone. The long downpour of the heart. Water in the valley like many dreams running side by side in long evenings of water, the moon hidden in the radiant mists, like a lodestone in its visible magnetism, the garden like a great scented promise, a rainbow built of earth and wet. Two very old voices speak slowly from the sky. The ancient fortress of the moon resounds with its words. Old voices, sounding ever-young.

III.

Those bodies whose hair was burning in the fire received human shape, and felt and heard and walked, and in the smell and the smoke of their own hair, came and rapped at the doors. It is the nature of the fruit of the grapes of these vineyards to go down so sweetly as to cause the lips of them that are asleep to speak dreams. It was this psychiatrist's opinion that everything his patients told him was true.

Luminous Collar

I.

Her blouse opens like the bow-wave of a trim craft splitting open on briny depths and foamy vaults; so the small boat forages over the skinless skin of the ocean. Whether she stands in a lily or a rearing wave of the sea, I cannot at the moment tell. Her voice comes out of this flower. If she were naked like Botticelli's Venus, so many fine points would be invisible. Just now I notice how a fine white daylight is shed upwards as from a snowfield by the smooth lapping of her collar. This radiance whitens her teeth and reddens her smile and flashes her eyes. In addition, the countenance is extended downwards in a Vee where two pillars like restless brides stand guard over the smooth trachea whose voice-box is almost imperceptible; it is maybe to show this sexual difference and to tease us with it that the collar is not merely left open but constructed to reveal. I have to repeat in a whisper that these clothes are also modelled like the female genitals in disguise with their folds and their introit. I feel she has tuned to one of the persons she is by choosing her collar like two birdwhite bones; it is easy to feel the touch of air on the carotid plexus in empathy with the touch just of her collar-bone on the soft blouse. As she moves she shapes a certain breeze escaping from short sleeves and neck, and this breeze opens by its touch and perfume briny depths and rosy vaults in the dead-white blouse.

II.

Familiar mysticism, living with the women by the field of wheat at Budock. That sea of wheat, the bands of shadows gliding across it from the road to the footpath that they cross secretly. She walks by it with her throat bare, familiar; a luminous vulva folded of cloth at her throat, pretending it is not that. Visible everywhere, in the hot weather that discloses. The women maintain their power by their symbolism, which is power and joy. The string of black beads like dark moons taps against the luminous collar, like a small overture, ripening. Speech rises and mingles with emissions from this flue in warm convection, filling living-rooms, or uncoiling down the path, mingling with the wheat, in the air one flesh, volatile; in solitude an invisible companion for conversation; in company, deepening; on the footpath speaking with the speaking wheat of bread and harvest. She smiles at me just as if all this were going on, which it is, whether the eyes are shut or open, even if there are no eyes but only skin. And across their tea-tables mingling scents of breath, cream, tea, jam, bread. In such places we must speak fair words to the sweetsmelling; the font is inexhaustible.

The Old Horse Pond

The old horsepond in the Sigmund-Platz. I think of the swarming of the bees as the Mass of the Bees. We set the oldest table in the yard with our best plates, and the sky bent down and helped our table to a meal of hail. The fritillaried path was still fritillaried, being under shelter. We brushed the small ice off awaiting the arrival of the Lord and Master in his feudal belt. Why, a nightflying moth settled on his plate like a double-window open on stars.

Shame and sweetness bow before the Master – his party bow tie is like a hovering moth with spots. Feelings of light beat wings in my sacrum when I see him; he says I make him sleepy; it is that dynamo which sends sleep-currents into the air. Why, as he spoke, I thought the Master still alive in his belt and bow. It was the sight of that black-and-silver-spotted moth settled on his plate, looking so like his tie, and I felt the shame and sweetness with which I knew him; that moth, looking like a free-flying black poppy flapped its wings a little as if the Master were adjusting his tie – beating its sleep-currents in the beautiful green caverns of the Sigmund-Platz, so fruitful that it was as though the peaches piled on shelves. There were many other old women bent like fruitful peach trees tending the master's fragmentary appearances in the arbours of the Sigmund-Platz today, despite the showers of hail, under the broad spans of many rainbows.

Work

He does it in this room draughty and full of light, like composing on the decks of a yacht plying a sunny sea, but what of that? An individual carries his dark and light within, and his yacht to unknown regions. And is also one who may decide for himself whether with whisky to separate the evening from the day without, and the light powers from the dark, within.

Therefore it matters not at all, for his music, or anything else, that the railway tunnel plunges into dark, like an entry into caves. He looks up at the inside dark span stubbled white with small stalactites laced out of the brick – a single drop of water winks feeble light at the shelly tip of one, like a single candle-flame burning upside-down. He walks on into sudden rain at the further tunnel-end, and through rain, which matters not at all to music or to anything, but is wet, so he turns back into the sheltering darkness, again looks up. Now the shower has lighted up an entire stone-candle forest, prisming the whole swoop of the sooty ceiling: the lower inside sky of the dank brick arch, railway become rainbow arching his walk.

The water that leaches through the courses of brick accretes over the years these tubes around its course, at the points of which it burns rainbows in the slanted sunshine of evening and morning. These industrial though wholly natural stalactites resembling caddis-tubes are of course sunlight detectors. The rays which pierce into the tunnel from the north-east at dawn or at sunset from the south-west, would do so unseen without the presence of pendent water, and fade away into the gloom of the tunnel. It is as this string quartet fiddling through the radio air would pass unnoticed were it not for the resonating span of that transistor set; just as its mineral rectifiers are tuned to a certain proportion, so the light caught in that hanging drop cracks into chords of small rainbows, lingering. And so it is with his high draughty room.

In this room beating with draughty light, he works without whisky at his music, as though speeding across seas that could not be seen or heard if he were not working; navigating at speed through sunlit equanimities and past wiry long spume that pounds off coasts his music makes audible.

The Wedding

This neighbourhood is belled by its church as a cat is belled to warn the sinless mice that black pussy-thunder is on its way; sin stalks through the town and you can hear it coming. It was after the wedding that the bells struck up, and the people swarmed out in their nuptial white and black because there was not enough room inside for both them and that symphony of bells. But then it was the Chimp in the Champagne that made all the trees gibber and scratch their armpits and the wind veered and there were fewer bells in the wind; cry blessing to the Chimps in the Champerzoo. Who caught the posy? There was a bridesmaid – and one tear fills immensity. After sin-eating in the bronze-voiced tabernacle she delayed because she saw an Atlas-moth settled on a lichened stone, with all the countries of the world marked on its wings, and the name on the stone was the name of the bridegroom lost to her: THUNDER-STONE. Then on to the reception, where the wind had veered again and pressed into all the bottles and glasses, flattening the champagne so thin that it could hardly be lifted; you could see its tones treading the lake, like the prints of a later wedding-party, an alternative outcome.

The Voice of Splitting Open

The voice of splitting-open, the thunder-sac full of water and noise. The tree in the rain dripping like a wet-nurse. The evergreen tree of dawn that rises raining from the waters of night. It was weather from the East that attacked us, climaxed and changed, producing a salty post-coital mist everywhere. She had been awake in the night, aching like a piano in dis-chord. Now she was vigorously scouring the depths of her blackest pot. There was a field of electricity, as if an electrified replica of our house had fitted over the usual one, and this mansion was furnished in semi-visible colours that plucked unexpectedly at our eyes, and populous with strange extensions of our ordinary senses, particularly touch. She was scouring her pot in search of those colours, I suspected; and the cat surprised me by having so much established his place on my shoulder with his vibrant warmth that when he jumped off I felt a territorial ghost cat sitting there still exerting its pressure. There were many other participants affected by the weather, momentarily possessed or nudged out of their usual track. Who is this who is coming through the dripping trees, a wanderer dressed in a shining bear's skin and singing a song of three notes?

The Tigers

The light condenses into its proper fruits. There is an arcade of lanterns, lampions in the Chinese fashion. Mandarins glide through the silky grasses, and Chinese tigers. The grasses, taller than the mandarins, shed light out of their fruits and from their yonis of dew. With the light they shed incense. The mandarins pause, and snuff up the religious odour, and then run on, pursued by the tigers through the striped grasses. And the tigers pause, to snuff up the spoor of mandarin-meat, then run on, pursued by mandarins with bows and arrows. The sound is of silks whistling. The silky stems, the robes of emerald green, the striped growling of the tigers as they stalk between the stems on which the huge dews pause, not quivering.

Then after the mandarins have finished with the tigers and the tigers with the mandarins the peaceable outriders come and with their scimitars they fell the grasses which drop and bleed hay-funeral incense and extraordinary balsams, they clear away the bones of mandarin and of tiger intermingled in their silken nets, bones enamelled with blood and grass-balsam – a most potent medicine for the male – and they weave the flax of the grasses into perfumed mandarins' caps which they wear to stalk tigers through gigantic savannahs for their crop of blood and bones and vegetable balsam.

Science

Science is common-sense, regimented. We've had enough of that – let us have uncommon sense unleashed. A comet hatches in the closed furnace. The breath of the comet passes through our walls. The infinitesimal black hole which is its head passes from one window to the other of the mead-hall, out into the black night; its tail follows, drawing endlessly through the windows. The mists are more golden for their suffusion with the comet's electricity, the blondes blonder, the wheat taller, the battles bloodier, the peace more uncertain; yet prodigies are seen, they say, in the heads of sages: look into her dark eyes and see the comet flies there as well. Women with no pretension to sagehood groom their hair into comet-shapes, their clothes are studded with sequins in sequences of shooting stars. The comet's bright head is moulded of ice and tar. In what closed furnace was it hatched? In her own furnace. This familiar room transformed by the sleeping body. Regarding it, he pours two glasses of the Beaune laid down in the year of the comet.

A Delicious Halva

I held suspended from a thread in my right hand a small tower of eagles constructed from an arrangement of discs. Under the copper dome this instrument began to vibrate and send out threads, like a spinning of gossamer. Whatever had stopped me proceeding further into the building lifted its influence and I walked slowly in. There was a carpet under my feet of eagle and tower motifs; the discs were shown with undulant threads being thrown off and weaving into the carpet's own pile. At the end of the hall was a table laid for dinner. I walked up some steps and inspected the covers. The cutlery was embossed with eagle and tower motifs. I did not sit down as I did not yet know whether I was here to eat or serve. There was a large ivory box in the centre of the table. I opened it. Inside, wrapped in leaves was a lump of greyish-brown material dusted with a powder. I could not resist taking a crumb. It was a delicious halva. I wanted to take the risk that the natural hormones alone of the sesame-seeds and rosewater it contained were acting upon me, and that the dusting was not a drug, heroin or cocaine, for the one crumb had made the substance indispensible to my mouth, which had become like a restless bed until more of its consort had entered it. I had put my instruments on the table; their vibration was now transferred to the taste of the halva, which was spinning threads of sensation through my whole body. I ate; I was here to eat, and then to serve. I had entered this hall in the perfect calm knowledge of the princess who had fed on nothing but sesame seeds and drunk nothing but water, and who was the sole source of the supreme halva.

97

The Pledge

A pub of ruinous ornaments, music and light, and quick continual movement, like walking into a decorated Christmas Tree, deep green, a smell of pine, and glitter everywhere. At the piano, he hurled the sonatas away from him. 'It's no use getting drunk tonight,' he cried, 'we must stay alert! The blood of the womb is still upon us all. You cannot wash it away with beer. You must stand fast through the night.' The roar of the lion rolled across the lit up bay from the zoo in the park.

The Path

The brimstone full of its aspect. A fragility of tenure among the bolts of sulphur; deep in the yellow mine, an accidie. The molten element has set in gulf-like heiroglyphs. Her guards lay dead and her clothes dripped blood. 'Let us hide in the sulphur mines,' she said, and handed him a lamp. They walked through the great wooden doors into the cellar as if they were beating a path into the sun.

At Sennen

All she could see was two gently-waving fields of tall grass. Science and love bring the universe close. The woman tied her boy's hair with a hankie. She heard a Latin scream, so she brought him a cup of hot chocolate to warm his writing. He thanked her in his duty-voice. The night was touched with the sudden September cold. Mrs Oldmist had shown her a garden of ancient roses; her first period had come and the old lady unlocked the door, and they both went in. She did not know whether the rose-red shone more within or without.

Ad Marginem

A round, dark, dew-encircled house. A company of men on the edge of monstrous putrefactions, dwellers by the mud-flats which are speckled by pure white birds. A fishing-boat nosing through the currents. A head of Kant in the misty window. One merely crouching down in the furrows to smell the turned earth, memorising its perfume; another student-lover crushing a grape between finger and thumb, next a bunch of them in the fist so that the juice runs down, then an egg in each hand so they spurt gold through all the fingers, simultaneously squeezing the opulent mud through his toes, then linking the two hands and bursting an apple, rubbing the pulp over the forehead, trampling up and down, inhaling the breezes imprisoned in earth, grape, egg, apple, self.

After the Funeral

A huge rainwater gargoyle with the face of a horse. Putting one's mouth to the cold, sweet flute in the rainy graveyard for the funeral of an old woman whose cheeks were cool and fragrant to kiss and whose robes always smelled faintly of lily of the valley. Afterwards, tea, in the huge gargoyle of a house with its chairs of a deep raisin colour. I was upset, distressed, but a remark made by my partner cheered me. She was staring at the chairs. 'Raisin,' she said, 'Raisin' up,' and she giggled, 'Resurrection, a sign!' and she waved her arm around her head. A distinct odour of lily of the valley came from her armpit, and I wondered whether smells were inherited.

Astral Bedrooms

A mislaid symbolism begins to collect dreams once more. The snail builds its staircase by rolling over and over. The single room in the hotel is as slender as his penis. The double room is deep and secret as a well, an L-shaped well full of astral water. The sea visits. The full moon is perched at the crest of the hill like a snowball ready to roll down, enlarging as it descends. The Seven Stars is open already, and Orion strides above with all his luminaries busy as drinkers' throats; and the great Hotel, riding the night like an ornamental galleon, why, its beds will be full tonight, and they will be busily working, and the sky above will be packed with twinkling stars, as though all the astral bodies of the guests had been connected to their roots above in the constellations, by their practice of sex. Each bed is a white star, fluttering. And be it known that stars flow through the rocks as the wind rises and presses on the land, the air pressed upon by the stars' action.

Sunday Walk of the Alchemist

Deep soft collisions in the air. Like a haunted train. Haunted by the exquisite beauty of the materials. Not casual and not opportunistic. The sacramental function of suffering projected on to matter itself. The black and white threads pulsing in the loom. You and your magic sound created by the mere fact of the body working. For everything on earth has its sferics. I hear a ghostly picture of your vulva unfolding. A womb-sound surrounds us. The barks of the trees are wet and running with wet like enormous alchemical vessels. Weather-response spells out a tree-alphabet. The rising and setting of planets spell out their creatures on the earth. Here, in this wood's centre a great stone, with apple, ash and holly. They make a womb-sound like a vulva unfolding, spelled CNT. Ah, that's it, the registration number of the car that brought us here. CNT 666F.

Anamnesis

The climax is simultaneous: the orgasm supervening over the next few hours – a kind of sensitive hyperbole, a firmness of carriage and belly, a contemplation sustained by an awareness of the whole skin and, because it is after all day fifteen of her cycle, a slight show of blood after an evening shit. It was not buttons he had feared, it was the moon's cycle. The pearly buttons with their four holes for thread stated aloud the moon's circulation with its stations and its influences here below. And so the sadness of being a woman alone soaked out of his grandma's shirt, wriggling through the buttonholes, past the buttons, which glowed with disappointed passion. When it lay soaking in the basin, the limp shirt pouting its buttons like little flat warts was the saddest and most disappointed garment he had ever seen. Then his earliest memory arrived. It was a fairy story told to him, read from a book with coloured illustrations. The king was incensed because he repeatedly found a button in his daily puddings. How that revolted our post-orgasmic contemplative. To get such a thing in one's mouth, like the crust of some spider. A pearly button with a reverse side freckled or stained by what emissions! It was like kissing the face and finding it was a cuttlebone mask. Each shirt had six little nipple-simulacra and they gave him breakfast from a bottle cradled in a front great as a bloused bow-wave and decorated with barnacles, when he wanted mother!

In the same story, he now remembered that the king on his walk had found pieces of blue sky that had shattered from the dome and had fallen on the broad path, and sparkled there with a few bright frosty stars still flashing. Simultaneously the king found a moon in his mouth, which tasted of blood.

The Duct

The summer lets its order open. The coffins float upon a sea which is the final reservoir of those waters which began in the robe of the High Priestess. A most wonderful fluid, which is full of eyes. How the blessed waters come down and look at the dead in the underworld! Look how the elixir of life enters them and how they are woken up so they come out of their beds! The light smiled silently in the aethyr, its home, down past the tree-top chicane. The house has more than a thousand doors through which the light from the celestial regions can shine.

They set images of fright to frighten the frightful. There were lovely maidens, white-haired from childhood. The banquet shared which is also a translation of form: the loaves, the butter, the meat changed into white hair. We know the ever-risen wind which is also a ghost; but has our friend laid sufficient hold on life to live again in death? Does he know the words for removing displeasure from the heart of the Judge of the Dead? He who knows the word on earth and has it written on his coffin will be able to go in and out by day under any form he chooses in which he can penetrate his dwelling-place and also make his way to the fields of peace and plenty. As a beetle or serpent he passed through the solid earth, as a crocodile through the water, as a hawk through the air, as a jackal or cat he saw in the dark – he of the nose; as an ibis he was a knowing one. The shades live! They have raised their powers! I have carried off and put together my forms by harmonic telegraphy; I make my ugly face at you if it happens you are doing wrong; for you if it chances that you are doing right.

My cells perfumed with marvellous wine! Everything temporal is only a simile. They will be drunk from the overflow of thine house, fluid intoxication between the sexes, a certain chemistry. Thus the lovers bear the beloveds in a particular way in their blood. They have in their house a rock which is also a well, in it takes place the vision of the fullness of sun and moon, the fetters of darkness and dumbness drop off in its beds, then eyes have been given to me and I am glorified through them, all my fluids perfumed with marvellous wine. In that rock, the feeling of union with a limitless substance, or in that well, the Cypress Quartet playing on Radio Three, timing ourselves to their soft deep percussions, as in the secret chamber the unexpected happening is forged in the iron of blood.

The enfolding robe falls on the soft resting-place, and the sweet hypocaust is lit. When her image came to me in the night, the fright almost killed me. The spasm is a momentary incursion into the realm of death; it is an example granted by nature to the being who is alive. Coitus consists of two people hurling themselves into death but with the ability to return, to live and to remember. The divine symbol of the Supper is an enigma for earthly senses, but he who has once drawn the breath of life from an ardent beloved mouth and whose eye is opened will eat of his own body and drink of his own blood forever.

A Forest of Invisibles

I.

Alive and gliding loosely down the street on my bike: on the
right the cattle-pit, the great black gash in the green field
streaked with lime and disinfectants. An old man in a white
laboratory coat was driving the cattle with a withy through a
milky pool. They had blisters on their poor dumb muzzles.
Three long black cars with one-way windows were waved
through the road-block without examination; I wafted through
on my push-bike and the old man in the field shook his stick
at me as though I were an errant calf.

II.

He carried great iron nails in his hands across the church pathway; these were his dowsing rods, and I saw them swing very
blackly as he crossed a line. My pendulum was a holed pebble
on a string, and it gyrated at one point on the path, there, and
nowhere else. A centre? he suggested, and so it appeared. A
small centre in line with the font and the altar. I remarked that
I had not dowsed for some years. He said, don't be nervous,
they love to be called up; we call them by taking out our pen-
dulums and they love to rise like dolphins leaping to show us
the mysteries. We walked back through a forest of invisibles
who wished us to know them.

III.

In the process of the seasons the adept and his chemicals suf-
fer the mortification known as the Dead Moth Tango. The
stars roll overhead like crystals in the stone cylinders of steam-
rollers compelling a road to be flat and fair. Alchemy is the

astrology of earth, and the arts of embalmment and of rending the tomb. Metals are alive like ourselves; the constellations grazing our atmosphere create the fragrance of certain named perfumes; and hence proceed wonders, which are here established. The visible world becomes like a tapestry stirred by stellar perfumes on the winds behind it. A slowworm thrashes on the smooth path; I slide him gently into the grass verge and the green fire which will give him purchase. In the orchard a ginger cat dabs with its sheathed paw at a green apple which is full to the core of gold and black wasps.

The Villanelle of the Little Duck

I.

A very subtle deepening over and above the sensation and the pang which made itself felt principally in my neck, a couple of inches below my ears, where the bony part stops. Is this where the Eustachian tubes are embedded, or the carotid plexus stells? As I deepened into it I met poor PV's bankruptcy ascending, but I switched off recollection and floated down past it without touching or adhering. Tat was asleep. Having woken and got up, I looked over the banisters and noticed that my magical walking-stick had become magical. But it is February winter, and the green, even the traces of January, that hue and spirit, has now and for the whole of this month sunk out of sight, the Cornish Persephone not being expected for at least eight long weeks more. Where does my stick want to go?

II.

In the green room, with ginger hair. She has her arm in a plaster cast, and she has carefully lacquered her nails scarlet, because the cat was so ginger on his green. He stretched his back on the green grass and looked at her goldenly. He was a blood-eater in the wide green: a mere mouse, headless in a green thicket, so red a lamb within the green, its head elsewhere. Ginger sizzling on the green rises and to the thicket paces to taste the headlessness and the red with the ginger of itself. The patient watches from her bed the greenness of the lawn gingered by the cat playing with scarlet.

III.

'The villanelle of the little duck…' He stopped writing for a
moment and turned into a stone over which the brook flowed
and hunched its garment cool around his neck, and a rainbow
cracked out of its collar. A stone. Already. The quiet thrum of
water shook the rainbow. A butterfly sip sip investigated the
stone for a bead of water. I found one in my own eye, turned
my head and offered the eye like a flower to the butterfly. The
villanelle of the little duck. I had particularly enjoyed the Hall
of Ships, into which they had got the Queen Mary, dry. As
we were returning, on the station platform in the crowd,
there was a woman with a pram. Her baby was fiddling with
some typewritten documents. Suddenly and with a seraphic
smile the child handed me a sheaf of them, headed RESEARCH
SOLUTIONS. The woman smiled at me and wiped a tear away.

IV.

Myself and another man had mastered our periods. We had
done this by tucking a large folio book under our arms, each
of us. It was the colour and pattern of a handkerchief that had
been used for a nosebleed, quite slim, but with large pages,
like a sketchbook, elephant size, that looked tie-dyed. Previous
to this we had suffered badly from PMT, which was like a
large white empty space, a marquee made of an immense
rubber, inside which one could not breathe, and felt spiky and
glittering, in the swollen stance of snowmen. Now however
we did not have to worry about this, since we had our blood-
stained books. Now it was a simple matter to join any company; I went into a meeting of playwrights, and we got on
very well.

A Certain Verderer

More sunlight penetrates the oak trees than it does any other timber. A certain verderer of the New Forest contemplates the Western Hemlock – its graceful drooping habit throws off the heavy snowfalls among the naked pillars of Douglas Fir – in the snooze of the adder, the trance of the grass-snake, in the litter of inner bark marked with benzene rings, its hexagonal lining. In Silesia the Sunday after Laetare is called Dead Sunday. Or Summer Sunday and it is on that day that 'Death' is carried. 'Death' is a doll. That is in their forests. Here, the adder wakes, the smooth snake-leather squeaking-clean as she passes in coils over the dead leaves – the rustling of her matches the rustling of leaves still on the tree, so by matched sound she is inaudible, by matched pattern she is invisible. The hiss is compiled by the wind tearing on the milliard tips of pine-needles. The wind having passed, all things in the forest play again in their preferred stillness. The tree-sound replays in the tree-scent, which its vibration has elicited; the latter is the silent mode. My stone cell is at a corner of the forest. When the wind blows from the west I can smell the pines, but only by standing on my bed and craning can I glimpse their towers. On waking this morning I found a pine cone on the window-sill. As I sniff it, the tree-sound replays in the scent, I dream-hear it, as though the cone were the shape of my trance, its crocodilian scales, its pineal origin. I see in the smell the blue haze between the naked pillars of the forest, sniff and comprehend their balsamic transactions. I will leave the cone on the sill; as the sun reaches it, the plates or wooden petals unfold like fingernails, tipped with red. My cell is now part of the forest, like a lair, and the roots of a great tree run within the stone blocks. The pine-cone is my clock. And when it shuts at night, my dreams will open the doors to me.

With This Wolf I Thee Wed

I.

I purr in my round stomach, I make room for the Khat there. Or it may clamber with its claws up the carved ivory ladder of my spine. It is black but all gold inside, its self, Selbst lives in a lighted room of gold with doorways, curtained doorways which are its eyes. The body you see is only the paw of the dreambody. It is a jet-coloured panther, I ride on it in a fur hat. Spirits have I. It has a crystal and a great comb in its mouth, the crystal drips clear, the black comb vibrates very deep. Seer and foreseer, sister of the serpent. The skin of a cat is my badge. The black and invisible fur of the Khat rises on my skin. Sometimes there is conflict, the cat dancing and dabbing out with his paw at the spiralling leaves. Gold eyes like the gold braid of a captain. It is an animal that lays gold eggs, the gold eggs are the eyes of its kittens.

II.

The broken gas-mains still burned at intervals along the flooded boulevards, like an underwater city of fire. Indeed that town was full of implicit fire at all times, blazing with radio waves. And they poisoned nature, so that the clouds ascended the heavens radiating fire on that high frequency that shatters us like the prolonged note of an intolerable god-voice. The skeletons fluoresce with it, and destroy the flesh of which they are platforms. In all the clouds was the bonfire of crushed radio.

III.

The shaman has to be sung to full size by his confessors in the place known as the clay pan of the moonlight. The town like a floating island moves away on the sunshine. He tells me this is God's hand on his lap, they are his fingers with the light shining in their clear nails, the bright cloud-sails above me, the air raining within the sails, the quest is to develop a good cut of sail, a suit of sails, the breath lingering, the peplum of the utterance pregnant with the wind; he says, moving his fingers only slightly, as though the clouds were attached to them on long strings, work coming from the deathless place will be deathless.

IV.

A gulf orgasm, altering the balance of senses. This was in the wooded village, where, because of this, I could see less but hear more. I heard the clouds overhead, like moving furniture, and the waters rushing away under my feet down invisible gulfs; the gulf orgasm opened gulfs: at night into the stars, and there was no limit here, hence the term: gulf orgasm. The rivers slanted, pouring down from their sources, conflowing with peals of thunder. But also my tree was in leaf in that village, where the wind exhales and calms us, inhales and tenses us. I heard the water-mains like the soughing of boughs, and this was because the pipes were hollowed-out elms. The trees were thickly planted along the boulevards to ensure a regular supply of under-water pipes, wheel-hubs and coffins; fountain-makers and boat-builders were eager for their elastic timber. In the village square there was a great fountain made of carved elm. From wooden spouts carved in guilloche spring eight jets that rise high in the air and feel back into an extensive wooden basin made from a three-hundred year old tree, the grain displaying all the echoes of its history.

V.

Young man holding in a pair of Alsatians on leashes, like holstered pistols fully-cocked, to the wedding. The breath of the young woman clouded in veils, her breath had the tang of cordite for the kiss in the White Opera, her wedding. The power animal bends the wedding wildfire in its tongue. With this wolf I thee wed.

The Electrical Man

I.

To electrify the air inside one's shirt by rubbing one's feet across the nylon carpet; to make one's electrical mark on the air by turning swiftly in a skirt, letting out a whirling ring or cool-plasma torus of the air of one's legs propelled by the vortical movement of the skirt; to sit down in a big armchair like a throne and to puff out this atmosphere from the garments like a ship settling among clouds of invisible ooze; these effects which can be felt but not seen enhanced by the odour of others' puzzlement and surprise, but oneself in the perfect poise of one's knowledge of them serenely strolling in the garden of one's garments, a flexible complex vessel always on the boil – in short, provocative, and always wearing the same thalamic smile. A smell like a curative herb-garden blooming from her thighs as she sits down, settling her skirt around the synaes-thetic spaces, the light on her figure like honey poured on silk. This system of electrical fields is an incredibly sensitive oscillator responding to field-changes in the weather, and is the sun, moon's and planets' machinery doing their business to and fro in the earth, and up and down it.

II.

'Arcaded walks stretching such distances that their lengths cannot be traversed in a single day…So lofty are the palaces that comets stream through their portals…' His concentration wrote the letters of his frown out on his brow; would he venture out to the halls of the comet today? Did they exist today? He observed a monster smoke at the top of the hill. Or would he stay perfectly still, hoarding electricity within the airy rooms of his garments, so that in the evening he would be a light to the world? To see or be seen; the choice was his.

Philosopher and Skin

I.

She had legs like earth-stairs. She spilt gravy into her lap. She sat in a written chair. I felt her wings flare out in her body like swooping Dracula. She was the night-side of the dove. I had drunk water fresh from a thunderstorm. Take a look in the mirror, Eden. Greeting the beasts by urine-gesture. Butterflies from the North.

II.

Leylines like stars with their rays reflected on the earth's surface. The craters on the Moon as if a hammer had been taken to a crystal ball. My body communicating its changes to my nose through the chimney of my clothes; I inhale these messages and return answers by sliding my changed saliva downwards. Plenty of wet girls in the mountains, clothed in goddess-skin of mist and waterfall.

III.

I smell my meal cooking. Its savour winds up through the Vee of her blouse. The anticipation of her skin makes me salivate. Winds up through the Vee of her blouse from the kitchens below, she ornaments this staircase with pearls. Through this white tunnel come the vaporous essays, the innocent alchemy. The pearl necklace hanging between the visible and invisible realms. The throat, the beach of invisible tides. The monthly laboratories, the pelvic silver beaten out. 'Ant' or 'Lizard' in her mouth greets the beast by inner gesture, 'Dog' with as close an approximation to the beast's smell as a human can give. Pretty close. Therefore are the beasts friendly.

IV.

Not an independent subject confronting an objective, alien world, but rather the so-called subjectivity, the ego or inner sanctum, and nature, and other people, and the whole world, emerge from a common ground, embracing both humans and nature. This state of fruitful death, the kore dwelling in both worlds, and passing from one to the other, dwelling also in the *Eidoleion*, the house of the future self. And reading, he understood that God was the ground of being: 'The ground. That's it! God is the ground!' looking out at the trees, and at the fresh rain soaking into God.

The Path Between Reality and the Soul

I.

The science of houses. Wandering veins of chemical colour running in all directions, including the directions of time. A visit to the homunculus workshop. A vine trailing from a thousand-foot peak. A vision half-sleeping with agate under the tongue. 'I'm Breakthrough' said a little girl carrying flowers. The spinal column turns into a magnificent road of ascent to a range of magical mountains which rise beyond the bony gates of the head. The breath this skull-foetus breathes comes from the beyond.

II.

The afternoon thunderstorms. All night we could hear birds passing. She read Greek aloud in the forest. It did not diminish her bordello radiance. Then she translated the passage: 'After his death, Pythagoras' house was turned into a shrine of Demeter.' There was a great shadow flitting under the sea. A ghost parking. There were invisible demands in the creaming March winds, everyone passing into transformation after their fashion – mother, cow, flowering hills.

III.

The path between reality and the soul. Who holdeth the seven stars in her hand, which are the seven spirits. A felled tree-stump; I smelled it and a face formed for a moment, a black and green face, and I said 'Spirits, let me know more of you'. The big elm had fallen across the flower-pots and shattered them. Its light-coloured wood under the powdery dark bark had split open into voids, attics and lofts, which were scented with the tree's dryad. I sniffed, and saw a tall and mobile fountain. I sniffed again, and saw a slender copse of trees which was at the same time a reverend old lady.

IV.

Anything fastened to the body, or floating on the ocean, is a counterfeit or an image of eternity. April: all behave like the flowers and the birds, old men climb their houses with flower-bright paintbrushes in their hands. A beetle shoots across the water-surface, shining with its waxes: it is a word. By moving through the house she wraps it in her coils of perfume: house-with-woman is a word. After his bath he wraps himself in a robe loose and blue as the sky.

Dr Lucky

I.

He is not a genius. He has a genius. Forgive me father, for I have sinned. Crouched in the confessional. A strong colour of aniseed. Crouched like a monkey in its cage. Father, I wish to walk tall. Make a good confession, then. I know the priest's name. Father Thomas Genius. Do you imagine you are special? He will give absolution to anyone who comes, providing they make a penance. To know when the windows of heaven are open, and when they are shut. We mustn't try to open them, or shut them; it is too serious a business to be left to humans. I had this patient with the ingrowing toenail. The hallux was inflamed, it is quite a simple surgical operation, or one may freeze with liquid nitrogen. He shuddered as I spoke, he shuddered as he came in and saw me. I have a large wart on my neck, like a toad. It is harmless, and useful to outface and comfort patients who are nervous about such things as growths. After all, I am perfectly healthy. The yellowish horny toe was twining downwards, as I have read the sacrificial boars of Malecula grow long spiralling tusks, created by knocking out a lower tooth which would have checked by grinding the descending tusk. I paused, said wait a moment, and looked for the homoeopathic remedy. It was Mag. Pol. Aust. Like cures like. It was as if his nail were being drawn like a lodestone to the antipodes. Very reasonable. Weeks later, I met him in the street. He was effusively grateful. The magic worked. He walked tall. He had been absolved of his nail. Genius had spoken through the Australian Lodestone. Why are the doors not always open?

The wart like a jewel on my neck. I have seen those who have long been dead, walking adorned with the clothes and the jewels which their friends had buried with them, who had formed an association for feeding the dead. My piety in the silence. I wonder if the priest on the other side has gone to sleep. So I became a doctor of the dead, curing, it seems, by magic poisons, and a toad in my sleep. The blue-eyed toad. Perched just below my left ear.

All things become of moment. My suit must take part in the healing process. Magenta wart, blue suit. Vest.med. Ground up, and distributed in sugar pills. Even my despised blue suit has its charm. This town needs me.

II.

There are many kinds of savages without gods, but none without ghosts, and none without doctors. I will take my magic charm or word of power from every place or thing in which it exists, and from which it runs about. Its genius.

I was never a catholic. Must I use that imagery? What is on the other side of the partition, the grille. A blue-eyed toad, for all I know. It touched me on the neck just below the ear, with its claw. Don't worry, they said, nobody will notice. And, it's not all that large, you know. For a little while I used grease-paint to cover it up. Now it is a part of my character. Why do I associate it with that confessional grille, that partition beyond which the magic sits, through which flows the odour of aniseed and magic? This tissue gives useful fancies. It has its genius.

The town looks like a single street of shops, of no particular note. A few older houses, on a hill a manor, and a church. But that is deceptive. The manor house had vast orchards, which were sold off, plot by plot, for building land. In the orchards grew good Edwardian houses, with turrets and libraries. I inherited one of these houses, in the orchards on the edge of the forest. My surgery is in the line of shops. I walk through orchards to get to work.

I miss the sea, a little. The blue springs of the sea, the grey fountains, the sailing mists and squalls. Often I dress in its colours. But always with a green tie. Or a bark-brown one.

IIII.

I wonder where Sway has got to, the moving town. There was a mansion there, and living in it a young man who never grew old. But the town shifted. I am looking back on my life, rummaging in my father's papers. I find a notebook labelled 'Hints to Parents'. It contains many kinds of note. I cannot make out whether this one, for instance, is a note for creative writing, or how my father became a doctor, my grandfather too; or perhaps it was how I became one; or all of us did. I never found a lady doctor who suited me, though the words 'lady doctor' are a powerful aphrodisiac. My father's, or my grandfather's, note ran as follows: 'If they discover that a boy can see spirits, they advise that he should be brought up in the medical profession, but as a man of mental medicine, who knows the mesmeric fluid. It is the ichor of the Gods, and that lake of life to which all go to draw their energies. Let them be taught all dressed in white, like proper doctors. Let them learn, still, without speaking, like chaste and wondering statues. The doctor may perceive the lake in any of these forms: a pentacle starfish, a star-of-David daffodil, a plate with a bread roll resting light as a feather on the heavy pewter, the roar of the baker's oven, and the tiny loaves swelling their breasts on his shovel, new-born baps; or in every or any pebble of the seashore: each one a corridor of power which sounds the hiss of their pouring scree. These also are the spirits.' One day I saw that my waiting-room was full of spirits: the paperweight with a painting of Margate, the cast-iron doorstop, the vase of daffodils, the empty chairs and sofa, for no other patients had arrived yet.

IV.

Near Bisterne there are two Dragon Fields, and nearby there is the Green Dragon Inn at Brook. The place is full of tumuli and Castles that have gone. All of these, I suppose, have genius, are full of the mesmeric fluid. I thought it right to fast, for if the foods have genius of various kind, that is a confusion within, of assimilation. If you can empty yourself out, then you are a starry vacuum. Unstop the evacuated container and a few molecules of genius rush in, like pure fresh air. So I fasted until I saw my future figured in the starry heavens, I mean, I saw the night sky as my coffin, the stars painted on the lid. It was my bier or birthplace. The seven stars whirled about the pole, which was the place I came in by, and the mooring place of the constellations. It was the natural of my heart, my mother; O, my heart, my mother, my beating heart of light…These words are the only ones I could find for what I saw there. As the acquired genius in me diminished, I saw the genius of the night sky pure. Then I brought myself back by placing a small piece of dry bread on my tongue. It is said to be the first moment of assimilation which bears the prophecy. The first touch on the tongue was like small snakes springing from a silver sleep. Small snakes of a busy nest under the tongue. It was as though the altar swarmed with snakes, dry shining and glistening snakes that were water distilled from the sheds of my skull. Like small snakes coiled in a busy sleep. I saw these by my own light.

I doubted whether Sir Moris Barkley of Beverston, Minstead and Brook killed the Dragon at all. I think he killed the man who saw dragons, the tiniest and most personal of which I have just myself seen, by a kind of dowsing of my mouth. I expect Sir Moris arises each time a seer is born, or created, a new Sir Moris, his antagonist. There is probably one such among my patients. I know it is a frequent fantasy among patients that they must kill their doctor in order to get well, and replace him as chief healer of the district. The police rang me this afternoon. There has been another murder in the district.

V.

It was in Bagnum Bog, a little east from Ringwood. A middle-aged man had apparently been stifled in a mud-hole. I think somebody or bodies had sat on his chest and forced his head backwards into the mud until he was drowned. At the autopsy his lungs were caked full of mud. Otherwise he was perfectly all right.

I got my first real kiss from my daughter today. She's a Caesarian child, and for a long time would not touch. She hated to touch or be touched by the various nannies who have taken care of her. There were screaming-fits until they learned better. Being a Caesarian child, she has a noble, symmetrical face, very handsome and undistorted by your common mortal's birth-trauma. I took her for a walk round the reservoir. She likes stamping in the puddles – no fear of touch there, her stockings were splashed up to the crotch. Then she said how she would like to get really dirty – not splashed, but slowly. She said she wished she was a pair of shoes, so she could get as dirty as shoes. I asked her why. She said it was fun. I tactfully agreed with her. No fear of touch here. I was surprised to find that I had a short stubby and very stiff erection, and my mind was full of images she had evoked. She's only nine. All that talk of touch, I expect, the touch of earth and water over the whole body, the freedom of breaking the taboo, evoked in her innocence. Then, over a kissing stile. She stopped the gate so I couldn't get through, and stretched her face upwards. I knew I was meant to kiss her, and so, for the first time, I did so. Strange that the same day brought the death by earth and water of that middle-aged stranger.

Last week I think it was, we went together into the foundations of the house. I had been showing some suspect pipes to the gas-man – they were old lead pipes that were fastened to the rafters by nails, and during the years the lead had flowed. The result was that the pipes dangled like wet spaghetti, and at places had bent almost to closure around the nail. These were to be replaced, and it would cost £109.50p. After he had gone, the trapdoor in the kitchen floor was still up. I asked Tess whether she would like to see under the house. To my surprise she was unafraid, and agreed. I said she would get dirty. She didn't mind. We clambered down the little tunnel into the foundations powdery with dust, littered with brick rubble. I found I could stand under the stairs. The foundations were flat stone, cemented higgledy piggledy together, like the stone walls of a dusty field. I found some contrivances of bent wire and rods which I knew were mole-traps. The torch-light made the stones and the rubble grey, like the crater of a moon. I let her go through a little archway which led under the back room, but only so far, as the opening was too small for me. She came back grinning. 'Is it so nice in there, then?' She nodded. Up a little slope of earth was a bigger arch. I looked into the underneaths of our front room where she had a lot of her toys and where we watched television. Yes, it was lovely, in its way. A little light came through the ventilation grating. The electric mains coiled in, like a black snake as thick as one of Tess's legs. The moony light made it a spare and spacious retreat, as for meditation among the simplicity of broken stone, dust, and dry light. I thought of how during the war this would have been converted to a shelter, where we would sleep. I hoped it would not be needed for that function ever again, for in atomic war it would be a cave refuge from the wild beasts that people would become. But no such use had ever been made of these foundations. They were untouched and vibrant in a kind of pure solitude, so seldom visited. When I look at my patients, sometimes, I see a kind of black shadow cast by their bodies. This is often just before they ask me a crucial question – about the thing which really worries them. It often puzzles me what this could be, and I took to calling it their 'genius'. I think it is the bloom of natural odour and warmth they give off while deciding whether to risk the question. I have noticed a similar effect when I have been massaging people, particularly up the spine. There are little blooms of heat blossoming to my touch. None of my books says anything about this. Eve, Tess's mother, used to produce similar shadows, very occasionally.

VI.

I look back at these pages and realise that the processes of change must be working very deeply so to involve a professional man in such curiosities and curious conjectures. Here in Hampshire we are tucked away from most social changes. It is Thatcher country, the heartland of this England. One can live in Agatha Christie country pretending that there is neither the atomic bomb nor Aids and not even except as an ancient whisper, Adolf Hitler. One can live one's life out in the enjoyments of one's personal visions or one's carefully cultivated energetic malice, like T.F. Powys' villagers. Nevertheless the changes springing from the decay of our age work like a curious yeast in the ovens of the mind, puffing up strange pastries. It is said that times of decadence, in order to give all the new energies their chance to emerge, are characterised by many kinds of curiosities, magic and witchcraft and sexual deviation and odd sports. I often think that computer games are exactly analogous to the hermetic memory exercises of the renaissance, theatres of memory. I read this morning of a famous poet who began his work by consulting the ouija board, and finished it by congratulating himself with a treat: a whiff of grass or a morsel of Alice B. Toklas fudge. Should I begin to use pendulum to diagnose my patients? Apply faith-healing? (the ulcer on Mrs Skinner's shin is healing slowly washed with nothing but a little Cetavlon. Nothing happened while she was doing it for herself; but when the doctor app-lied the same treatment, it began to heal.) Shall I perform operations under hypnosis? Whom shall I hypnotise, myself or the patient? And all these thoughts, are they not screening another matter? There was genius in Mrs Skinner's shin, to ulcerate itself to obtain a few minutes' harmless intimacy with her Doctor, a few wet kisses on the legs with a pad of cotton wool. What are my underthoughts? Or should I look for a song that deep? I think, quick, I see snakes again, but twined on a staff, natural image of a healer. But why now? Why not?

VII.

They say a physician is ripened by his art, but today I saw the mark of Cain upon one Skinner, a patient who had consulted me about migraines. It was not in the Surgery. I saw him through the window of the barber's. He sat in the chair like a murderer who would keep his dignity beyond death, sitting upright while the lightning played about his brows. Here it was the barber's scissors like metal birds building loose nests which slithered down the shoulders of this whiskerando in the barber's chair, shot like black sledges on the snow slopes of this wirehaired Stalin, rocky as Russia. I had a vision of fighting this man with great mallets. I pleaded with the exe-cutioner for reduced bouts as my opponent was younger than I, but he was implacable, and I realised it was a fight to the death. While he sat like a secret Florentine in his electrical chair, virile coarse hair sprayed about his shoulders. I looked for an explicit mark in the hair on the snowy cape forming and reforming like Hebrew letters, or Greek letters, or Chinese ones. My professional studies had not led me in this direction, and I did not know whether the mark of Cain signified a murderer accursed of God, or the mark of the one who was to be mur-dered by permission of God. Ah yes, it is the former: the mark of Cain means that no one can kill this man. His aura is des-olate and fills the little shop into which I shall not enter for my newspaper. He sullenly lids his eyes so that he shall not look directly at the one who cannot kill him.

What do I know about this Skinner? Age 33. Unmarried. Migraine. Went a week after my prescription. Not true migraine. Perhaps a pretext for talking to me. Lean jaw. Splendid thick black hair. Blue eyes. Blue five o'clock shadow. Teeth seem to be all his own. Blood pressure up. Urine normal. Handsome, yes, handsome. Took him for an actor. The kind of man Eve went for, when she didn't want me. It was either these plainly handsome husband-types, or old me, with my bit of medical mystery and my strange studies. Of course, I took them up because they were sexual to her, in certain moods. And to me. She still went off with a clean-limbed dull lover to have her other children. 'You can have Tess', she said, with a wave of her head. 'There's danger in her. You can have it.' Bitch.

VIII.

The name's not Skinner. It's Steiner. Skinner is the name of the old woman who likes me dabbing her ulcers. Maybe I should do it with my tongue, like a mediaeval saint. How could I have made that mistake; is it hardening of the arteries at only fifty? Steiner, Stoner, Stainer, Stainer's Mass or Requiem, getting stoned, stone walling, living stones, stone circles, witchcraft, sacrifices, cunning sacrificer, sacrifices to the Bog Goddess, losing one's head in the mud, one's life, spirits in the mud, murder by witchcraft, Pete Marsh, mute testimony, stones found in the marsh that were fastened to the bodies to stop them rising, memorial stones carved, saints in stone, up where I can see it.

I went to the Bog where the latest murder of the three had been discovered. I must follow these impulses, to find what they conceal. That is the essence of doctoring, the diseases I believe may be the threshold of genius, which from this side look like sickness. I think of the marsh as a reservoir of magnetic fluid, darkened with its power. I will simply rake any stone I can find in it up on to the shore and take it home, and carve it into whatever figure it suggests. Thus I will in an act of attention hold to the direction my psyche wishes to lead me. The light begins early, and I wanted to get there and back before anyone was stirring. The murderer returns to the scene of the crime – that was not a thought I wanted anybody to have. I drove to Burley and walked across Church moor. A great cloud was parked on the bog, like a multiple lorry. The grass everywhere is getting a bit yellow with autumn coming, and the trees are magnificently bruised, the rainbow of vegetable haematoma. I walked carefully into the fringes of the cloud, carrying my rake, testing the way with the handle. There is a lot of moss full of water which holds firm for a while and then begins to sink, wetting your shoes and slowly tinging with liquid mud. I could not at first find the firm ground from which the man had been smothered. When eventually I did I knelt there and pushed my rake deep into the mud lissom as pondwater. The white mist over the black reedy pool stared at me like a white blouse over a black skirt. My rake would not reach bottom, and I was too impatient to get up again and take my coat off, so I let my arm go in, overcoat and all, and touched bottom. It seemed smooth and oozy, with an occasional slight catch to it as the rake tines pulled a weed. Then it grated against stone. I knew it was too big to get up with the rake. I explored a little with the metal end, then pulled the implement out and laid it by my side on the firm turf. I laid down full-length and taking a deep breath I plunged the upper part of my body in the marsh as deep as I could go. My fingertips just got the stone and with an extra stretch and almost falling in completely I pulled the stone to me and hugging it to my chest wriggled back on to the grass, dripping with black. The stone was about the size of a woman's head, or a small man's.

IX.

I humped the stone across the moor back to the car. I had got what I came for, so there was no time to think about my clothes or the car seats. It looked like an alligator's cave when I got out. I had wrapped my overcoat round the stone and put it on the seat. Now I took it indoors and got into the bath, clothes and all with the wrapped stone on my belly, and turned the shower and the taps full on. Everything shone with water, wreathed in steam, and when the overcoat was sopping and rinsed of the best part of the mud, I unfolded it and watched the water play on the stone, turning it green.

As stones do when they're brought in from the wet sea-shore, the boulder shone bright green, and within the green there was a network of veining of darker green almost black, with small blotches or plaques of shady emerald. It looked like a demonstration in neurology done in botanical green, or stained in a vegetable dye. Suddenly I came to myself. What was a professional man doing in the bath with all his clothes on, his second-best doctor's suit, watching a shining green stone that sat on his lap. Then the door opened and Tess walked in. I had forgotten she was due to be taken to school this morning. She put her hand to her mouth, coughed politely, and left.

Later
It was not difficult to explain to Tess that I had been working out a dream that I could not otherwise remember. 'But in your *suit*, Daddy'. I said that when these impulses came to one one must not stop to change. She looked doubtful. We looked at the stone together. It was teatime. It was more like a head than I had remembered, a head, though, without a neck. The whole cranium, as it were, was smooth, and where the features and the ears would be was an irregular mass that was made of clustered prismatic forms. Dry, it shone less, but the stone had been mechanically polished, and had a gloss all over the 'skull', which enabled one to look into the interior. It looked like a door-stop I had seen in a Cornish house, made of a local serpentine stone. Yes, I believed it was serpentine. Tess thought so too, running her fingers over the mass of prisms. 'This looks like a mountain town, Daddy. I'm rather sorry it came out of the murdering pool. But I wish I had been there to help.'

X.

It's strange how a professional air attracts people's respectful greeting and smiles. I suppose that it's part of doctoring that the patients adopt a respectful, grateful air, even if they're private patients, and paying. After all, if I wasn't worth their respect, where would their money have gone? It's part of the healing fantasy. My confidence, rather than my diagnosis; my attitude rather than my treatment. I have noticed that my patients recently seem more than usually pleased with themselves. I am not accustomed to this radiation from patients. It

E

is they that seem to have the confidence now. Two remarkable things happened in surgery today. The first was with Steiner. He had lost his air of menace and become very civil.

How's the migraine, Mr Steiner? I can give you something stronger, if you wish.

No, no, it's gone. But I would like you to examine me.

Of course. I suppose the trouble has shifted somewhere else.

I'd rather you examined me before I said anything about that.

So I examined him thoroughly, and I have seldom seen a healthier man. I had noticed before some ankylosed joints, which I thought might give trouble later, and a slight inflammation in the throat, and slight adenoidal tenderness. His bloodpressure had been rather high for his age too. But there was nothing of that now. Reflexes, eyes, blood pressure, urine, all were pristine.

Well, Mr Steiner. I must congratulate you. You have a clean bill of health. In fact you are very healthy, and the slight troubles that sometimes go with the migraine have vanished!

I feel exceptionally well. I woke up feeling wonderful, and I still do. I wanted to be sure that it was there, too in my body, that wonderful ease that I've not felt since I was...

Six, maybe?

Since I was last in love.

The other remarkable thing was with Mrs Skinner, the lady with the ulcer on her shin. I was sponging it as usual, feeling a bit like Magdalen washing the feet of Christ, when she bent down and took hold of my hand.

'Doctor, would you just touch it with your fingers. That would be better'.

I stifled my proper scientific retort about that hardly being hygienic, and laid the pad of my thumb over the weeping sore, kneeling with one leg bent. Then without thinking I took my thumb away and quickly leaned down and kissed it. My tongue touched its centre. I don't know who was the more astonished myself, I think. I looked up at Mrs Skinner when I realised what I had done, and how she could get me struck off if she decided to make a fuss, but she had her eyes closed. Her face was bent to the ceiling and her lips pursed as though she were considering the sensation very carefully. I think she did not realise I had used my mouth. The taste was salty and slimy with a little sweetness. I swallowed. Mrs Skinner opened her eyes and looked at me. 'That's what it was asking for,' she murmured, and said nothing else as I put a light dressing on the place. Then, this also seemed natural and unpremeditated, she curtseyed and left.

Later

I felt a light tap on my shoulder as I was walking back from the newsagent with the Sundays. It was Mrs Skinner. She smiled and nodded. Crossing the road towards me was Steiner carrying a bunch of flowers, among a group of my other patients: I saw Standford the newsagent, the butcher, Charles, whose missing finger I had stitched when he lost it in the sawdust of his shop after an ill-aimed blow with his cleaver, Lady Cynthia, who was a real singer who had very bad chilblains, and my fellow-physician, Excott, junior partner of my rival, old Minges. Steiner handed the flowers to Mrs Skinner, who bobbed another curtsey and gave them to me. I took them, dumbfounded. I smiled and shook everybody's hand. I thought maybe they had mistaken my birthday. As I took the butcher's hand I took a quick look at my work on the forefinger joint. There was a small growth on the flat surface, I thought at first it was a long sturdy papilloma, in which case it would certainly need attention. Then I noticed the baby nail at its tip.

XI.

Today, Sunday, another unprecedented thing occurred, but this was so remarkable as to make the remarkable things that have happened so far like a mere portion of one's ordinary professional life. Tess was looking extra smart with her short red hair freshly washed and looking springy, like turf. I had to touch it several times to make sure it felt the way it looked; and then after this to tease her a little. We set off to Church in high spirits. I was wearing my best black go-to-funeral black suit. My second-best one was with the cleaner, who was doubtful about it. I was ashamed of its condition, of the mud. I had washed it through, though it said dry-cleaning only, and dried it in the tumble-dryer. I thought the wool-polyester might just survive and keep something of the original shape. My best suit was of quite another kind. Not off-the-peg, and made by a really expensive tailor. It felt good to be in. Its shape and warmth, its comforting weight, its waistcoat firm against my ribs, I was a professional silhouette, and felt strength and confidence from that. After all, it was my living.

We were a little late. The first hymn had started. We would slip in as best we could. Walking quietly we got nearly to our usual pew, without the sensation that we were behaving disrespectfully by coming in late. The hymn finished as we got to our seat, the organ stopped and everybody sat down just as we did. It was at that point that we seemed to be noticed. Heads were turning and craning. Then somebody started clapping, then more people joined in. Everybody stood up again and they were all looking at us and applauding. We struggled to our feet and looked round us and behind us, but there was no doubt – it was us they were clapping. To my astonishment the Vicar was walking up the aisle in his vestments, clapping. He stopped and cleared his throat, and took my hand in both of his and shook it warmly. Then he motioned me to precede him, gesturing that I was to go up towards the altar. In the din of applause he ushered me to the pulpit and nodded approvingly as I mounted. 'Just a few words, Dr Lucky' he whispered, 'just a few words before we begin to worship.' My fingers felt upward for the wart on my neck. They could not find it as I began speaking. I wish they would use the latin for my name. Faust. Dr Faust. More dignified.

❦ III.
IN THE ESPLUMEOR

An Alchemical Journal

Prologue

Somehow I had summoned a grave presence of great strength and truth. Dressed in a shift she went to the cupboard and brought out bright cheese. The great table was scrubbed white, and first we ate. Then we loved, where she spread the great white bolsters. She scattered crumbs for the birds. Returning her kindness those birds ate her plums. Grave presence, in that shift among the fruit trees. Great strength and truth treading with bare feet among the waspish cavernous plums. She was cavernous, but not waspish. She and the soft earth swarmed with liquors which felt. Among the trees hanging with ripe fruit, leaf-caverns bloomed and squeezed. The earth was wool-soft between the ancient boulders. When I came over the hill, that first night, I had walked too far, I knew nobody, but I had this address, the former wife of a former friend. I thought I had reached the sea, but it was the blue-grey slate roofs gleaming in the hollow. I knocked at the door, she was much smaller than I had expected, she had big hips and an impudent grin, long dark hair, a white shift. She said come in and poured me a glass of straw-coloured wine. There was a big hearth with a fire burning on it, and the smell of timber and stone, like a well. There was a big white wood table, and a recess piled with bolsters and eiderdowns. I was in that house for twelve weeks. On the one side I remember that I was there, and I can still taste the wine and feel the shape of the glass I drank out of that first night. On the other side of things, I cannot tell more than the edge of what we did and what we saw, though I kept a journal. Through that journal I can, by reading carefully, recover something of what occurred, something of what hides in the thickets of sensation. Those who have visited this house already will know my journal; they will have picked it up off the white table and have consulted it, for it is the only book that house allowed. Did I also mention that the woman of the house is black?

In the Esplumeor

You could watch the heat come off her skin like a tar road in August. She had become shack-sassy. He brought out a maj-olica humiodor, the gifted stranger, offering gifts. He could play the bottleneck like an angel, the neck of his white shirt sliced open like a wedding cake, on to his rich-fruit dark skin. Thus Wisdom changes hands among the wise. In an orchard of apple-trees, men and women huddle together, crying. The angel comes to comfort them.

Radar anomalies with heat, inversion layer – I listen to the mist and fog programmes on Radio Three. Height attacks lightning, as I hear the static that surrounds Sophocles like broken thorns. Under the mist, the mildly archaic water, the three men with long oars dipping, the coracle, an energumen, a cylinder of rain and pop music gliding like herding-calls.

A barber, whitened by age. You will never penetrate this, he averred, unless you know the keys of those doors. Oh? Doors? Odours. He adopted an obtuse walk to conceal his smell; but he had night eyes; like empty houses on a summer afternoon, they sent out the most marvellous implicit echoes. The tall slender mast comes straight at you across the water, straight towards the eye, the last snap of the sun flashes along the river. He took a swig of his flask of liquor, the old ignorant oil.

He was grateful for the building and approached its clear shrine. In it, he knew, was a great store of fine sea-sand, the sort that blows about and is used to fill hour-glasses. She came in after him; she wore a bracelet of repeating wings which covered her wrist; she found him standing looking at the great bunkers that contained the exquisite sand; the build-ing was the centre of an isolated grove of old trees of forest dimensions. She took his hand; 'I will show you where they keep the living oil,' she said.

His semen frozen for the future, into a jewel, such as that brooch of ivory she wears at her throat. Clothes as the patterns bodies make in time; her trailing hems electrify the whole room. A moon-suit, white on black, with frilly cuffs like tidal waves, diagrams the whole menstrual cycle. Gaslight in many jewels. As she rubbed my back, my shirt filled with light. She cast a glamour like a flare of light up from her throat over her face, and it shone like the brightest gold. Her perfume is her nature's self-homage. The dark girl with the straight back lifts the thick lenses of her glasses like chalices brimming with light.

The seven primary or fountain-spirits. All the stars are none other than the Goddess' powers. Renewal, coming of itself. The snake supposed to dwell in every fountain of the land. The cat's head full of magnetism. The croaking frog, a little sperm-fellow, a type of transformation. Choirs of frogs *underwater*; somehow their tune rises through the surface. Knots of frogs enjoying congress on lily-pads, scudding the sunshiny surface; pallid little fellows resting on the bottom ooze, exhausted.

He saw an affirming flame, it was a sign of approval, she had got a lie out of her hair, she had got the wrong breath out; after that, to stroke her skin like a cat's so it emits her perfume which combines with mine and fills the whole house with its radiance; and compounds with the radiance and perfume of the flowers, *lumen de lumine*, an electrochemical field, respirable gold, the fruits of the swift tree of life of the lightning, rooted in the sky, blossoming on earth.

A lowbrowed man in a white mess-jacket cocks his head at the sound of thunder in the snowstorm. The cold air instantly reeks of ozone and hot iron. There is another thunderclap so deep and intense that it seems to come through the hull from the abyss of ocean, and on up through the soles of the feet rattling the lights. The snowflakes are falling as fine as white sand and also in flopping mandalas big as ducks' feet. She comes up onto the deck like a great bush in bloom in her floral dressing-gown, and helps herself to scrambled egg yellow as daffodils. The steward bows, and offers her his favourite – kedgeree. Clothes in this ship are not like bits of a torn mask huddled together again every morning; they are a kind of abstract expressionism responsive to every mood. Thunder spreads from the steward's white front over the shoulders of his white jacket.

The cat's peppery smell, his sweat of hunting, his fish-breath, his primary catspaw dabbing at my hand; the gold lettering on ledgers like money showing through the cuts; the snaky shrines created by the geomants, around which the cats pad. Grabbing the snake and cracking the head off as one cracks a whip; the young man discovered it in the leather armchair, sewn into a cushion, waking out of its winter sleep. The mysterious nature of turbinal hiding-places, with their creeps and stumbling entrances, such tunnels; her scent multiplies the labyrinth for all creatures. But every woman brushes her hair out at the end of the day for a playback of the perfumes of events.

If the women were the brewers, both of social pints and strong ale to warm you to bed in the winter, they were bestowers thereby of gifts brought about by a resurrection of the spirit by fermentation out of dead things. Ale was a medicine. The American Indians were driven mad by secular rum, for the white man had forgotten that the visions and not the quantity of drink were of first importance. Such visions must be regulated by the women, as they regulate (according to the degree of their sorcery) the light bright fermentations from their own skins, continually changing bouquet with their mood and fertility, and the slight almost imperceptible electricity like an invisible hair or subtle pelt. Poison and medicine, soma, nectar, mead. Imparting gifts of the spirit to the men, for the women bled and lived, rising again among their fermentations; thus a drunken woman has had the light of her skin put out by some man. She can no longer credit her own distillments, and squats raving on a pile of shattered glass. But the sober mistress persuades him away from the pub by raising a slight intoxicating perfume from her own skin.

The healer's hand on my head, my meridians – Eden's circuits – going like express-trains, my navel glowing dream-grandeur. The substances are so dreamy. Am I dreaming, or manipulating, or being manipulated? To watch the supernatural films that play during the sex-act. To listen to a ghost-story on the radio half-asleep. The ghost-meditation: imagine that drops of a fluid are striking you – then wait for other messages by touch, if you dare. The great eyelashes sweeping the whole skin. The bones of clothes: the knuckle-buttons and the skeletons of seams. Undines, the wielders of fluids. An oven which is also a spring in a cave. We enter this great cave with the pendulous stalactite and we see far back in the wall the blunt cone shining black with wetness and fire. A big shining moves across the water, into the secret docks.

Then she closes the mirrors. Then she opens them. I felt her heart: it seemed to be beating *longer*, not faster; later she told me that when she came, there was an extraordinary warmth at her heart. Assorted dreams, I said, during her stray contractions, which were like spindles or flying saucers. Houses standing still like soldier spirits among the trembling trees. In stormy weather, when rings are tight. The strangler and the releaser: the channeller. What is open she closes, what is closed, she opens.

The bags under his eyes show that his kidneys are moving slowly into the next world. Resting from her five-act funeral. I remember how when the rain fell I entered another mental world. And how my grannie was just the visual form or mask of the atmosphere that filled the rooms of the house; in effect, each room made a different grannie, altered the mask slightly. Her skirts blew her about the house. And the younger woman: her magical suit, black as night, the open Vee of her blouse folded back on her jacket collar breathes at me, watches me, listens to me. Like the eye of the collar-bone a small pearl taps at the base of the throat, like a shell of the waters: she stirs her shoulders and her bosom rises and falls and like the sea the perfumed skin-air conches out. Like a conched ear the blouse spins down into its deep vaults where the heart taps out its massage message, creating perfume in those silk cellars.

Bricks make Staines, the small Roman bricks, fired parallel-epipeds of earth numerous as the leaves of a sober red forest; a Roman town occupying England – to see the small bricks again, to touch them, at the railway station, the trains rattling in and out, the bricks lasting, STAINES flatly stated in black-white on a tin notice like a banner of the forest-army; indeed, indeed, STAINES, I am here, it is warm for the bricks drink up the sunshine, it smells with tiny smells of red brick. There is more. It is the site of the great waterworks of London, and the Staines reservoirs like hammered pewter across which the wind blows, cooling, but the heart of the town is warm red brick. The artesians quaff continuously at the water-table, the water-table laid with the cutlery of great machines at the fringes of the forest of houses leaved with red bricks, small Roman bricks numerous as olive leaves, the sun shining like Roman fires, the streets hot as hypocausts; the under-fires of the earth lie hidden and responsive, the fire of the stars above lies hidden in our substances, the streets are made of star-stuff, the fire of our stars lies hidden in our habitations, in our fired Roman bricks.

A terrifying richness over the whole bay. An impression of silent thunder. My fire chaplain. The red veil. The sword turning each way. Sucking at the entrancing breath, at the trance-forming breast. Trial marriages, incorporating such customs as tarrying, night-visiting and courting-on-the-bed. The baker's whole establishment, years with that zest, his daughters, his ovens, his bed, the glowing sunset, crisp clouds like fresh baked bread rolls. I massage the daughter's feet; the mother-baker profits from her easy temper. And if the mother, I.

Skyclad, the stars over the skin, the skin as a celestial globe with the constellations intact; the black skin at night, with the eyes closed, and the hide gives off its night smell accordingly. The metals wafting off the river-mud like invisible foil unpeeling, shaking in silent thunder. Intricate circuit-breakers of the Docks lie open, 50 cycles per sec implicit only in after-echoes in the great resonating hulls. The disco on the wharf beating the anvil of perfume, as the thunder-anvil beats out its lightning with its own reverberations. A copper-galleon, beautifully beaten out thin to its function, the weather-vane twirls and the blind statue with the eyes chiselled to a blank stands staring into the sunset.

The door marked with the small male symbol, the weeny-phallus as a knocker. The three pale ladies wearing their prime punk gear, their widow fringes, towering eyebrows and bow-tied lips, collyrium in zombie circles under their eyes, knock his rapper. He saw no emnity in these faces, picking up his half-pint light as a kitten; the mothercat is a friend who undertakes to domesticate his garden, the Japanese bushes, the marble-dump. But dog, heavy, full of its turds, wags its tail down to its gut; his full pint, heavy as a dog wags his tail, wags its tail in his gut, the hounds of beer hunt inside him, their barking explodes in his farting anus like the belling of coursing hounds.

The two belly-passengers looked at each other. To wake from God. All thy garments smell of myrrh, and aloes, and cassia, out of the ivory palaces. Upon thy right hand stands the queen in gold of Ophir. The King's daughter is all glorious within; her clothing is of wrought gold. She has been brought in unto the King in raiment of needlework. The twins lifted their heads in her belly and regarded each other. Her belly was translucent like pearl. She ordered a lamp bright enough to cast the shadows of the twins through her bellyskin on to the white-washed wall. It was the golden dawn inside her. The twins had grown in the light you can see deep within the skin of a nude who is calm in reverie, when the lights of imperial purple and arterial scarlet mingle in the alchemical skin and shine golden. In this light, the twins regarded each other. Gold of Ophir.

The little horse in Killiow Gardens, her warmth glowed at me like coals, the chestnut glowed as I spoke to her, then she grew skittish and nearly knocked me down. I tuned into the glow from the pigs' flanks. In their orchard, their apple land of satisfaction, their grunts as round as fruit, their flanks built of opals, subterraning pigs, pork rooting under the apple, alas. The deserted dairy, with its dust of milk. The wagon-driver, on his celestial omnibus; as he named the trees, each stepped forward in its own perfume, the perfume sat down among us as we rode in two rows facing each other, the horse badged with symbols of fertility, golden brasses of wheatsheaves. I said 'steady' to the horse, and it stayed.

Irritations of the countryside: implicated by a pony, which dribbled on my vest. But later I was in milady's mouth at the centre of a silent round field, like the still centre of an EM torus. All revolved round this, and these: the study light of his neighbour weakening in the dawn, a night-time paralegal; the modest fortune he himself had acquired as a manufacturer of handbags; the young husband, his son, who said he could do as he pleased with other women because he had branded his flesh into his true and legal wife – he had marked her on her inner tissues with his red hot iron that would not be quenched; nor had he taken High John, the Conqueror Root.

By the Chinese Hand Laundry, 'Buy me a candle, Daddy'. A Seven Powers candle of multi-coloured indeed rainbow wax. Iris Del Arco watched a rainbow splash of oil oozing from under a bridge along the back of the river Frome. 'Such a candle burns for two weeks...' Watching a woman in a workshirt engaged in the homely art of cleaning paintbrushes, the room ablaze with gloss around her. Swabbing her hands with white spirit. A Chinese woman. In a clean room.

Young men could learn the secrets of magic by celebrating the sacred marriage, which is masturbating in the presence of the goddess' statue and ejecting semen upon it. Their shape-shifting then follows the phases of the moon. They can become wolves by passing through a certain magic pool, which is between the hills. They hear the hiss of the serpent as they push through the night-time foliage, and as they open the star-doors on their radio-sets.

She takes down the *Oxford Book of Ghost Stories*. By this I know her period is coming. Equally, I saw a hunchback consulting an angel: I saw this in a stain on her blouse as we were fucking. I suppose it was the same with her dog, only more so; he was examining with his nose some ort in the road, and the breeze blew; to him this would show speeding landscapes in a fine crystal. She came in from the rain as if her clothes were part of her, fused to her skin, like translucent gills. Pointing at a woman and saying 'You're wet!' is like pointing at a man's knobbly trouser-bulge. Accordingly he said it. Her sigh moved across his two hemispheres, uniting them. These matters belong to their confidential psalm. But he had the big head of a madman. The rain had stopped, and the blinds on the window stirred like the sails of a becalmed ship. As they finished, it rained again.

Organ music working from under the cliffs because of the water falling into sonorous caves, the rainwater heavy with limestone, water that leaves stone behind, the liquid sculptor seeking tiers to fringe and creating profound and immense organ consoles in blue-green marbling. There is an eye weeping on the cliff complete with lids, lashes and lenses where the water emerges. The cliff-face is an active or imaginal space like the easel of an artist painting pictures of the invisible lands within the cliff, the wild walls, forest walls, jungle walls with tigers, windscape walls with their clouds having interpreted the outside that became inside which becomes outside again carried away and laid down in the water – limewater writing on limestone a nine-foot wasp that must have impressed this artist since there it flies with tigerish stripes and a stalactite sting dripping with water cloudy as venom. Here is a lady off to the ball who on her way has removed from face under face a series of nine masks painted with ore-stains in swatches. As the sun goes down the artist will not stop work, while the cliff still playing its organ leans over us with its shadow like the dark subsonics vibrated in its lightless studios.

A minipractice of acupuncture – sticking pins in dollies – malign acupuncture. A book ripening like an apple, the natural alcohol stoked a warmth, a spell called 'restless oils'. The great hand that feels out the walls comes from the sleepwalker, lingers over Celestine's apple-pie. Sleeppower. The Saint has multiplied her hands. Every fabric, every thread of her drapery a nerve, feeling to each corner of the room as she descends. Nude descending, clothed in her vapours, her great power-sleeves, every space, even in the banal freshly-built house, full of grace felt out by her. With each stair a new set of feelers is created. Of wings. Her auric fields resemble a moth, if we did not know she was a nude descending we would think we were in the presence of a queen of moths and her perfumes that are lights. This gracious passing-through mediated by the odours. We do not need the invented pomps, each breath of air, each lungfull is a palace.

I saw her shorn of her glamour; I was privileged to see Duessa. This was because I had not reached puberty and the universe of her perfume that surrounded her did not touch my pre-sexual nature. Something to furnish her age and discontent could be provided by stories and phantasies. After that, the incest prohibition supervened, and she was a remote and glorious figure, or a close and glorious figure, but still the memories of that earlier scentless and non-hormonal vision of the pre-pubescent boy ripped away the tissue of glamour. Not so to the American soldier who passed the flask so hastily: he was a knight-errant. I have sought to clothe my odour by alchemy since. I saw the Duessa-nature early, and it was loving-kindly. Yet not so immune: she wished a kiss, the crone did: so I kissed her, and like a red hot poker plunged in a spicy drink, clouds of agreeable glamour surrounded her and altered her features and her speech. How beautiful she is, how beautiful, said all the men in love with her: but I knew better, and I knew she was better than beautiful: she was magic. It was my privilege to see her clothe and unclose herself in these garments and machineries of glamour, she was a perfect laboratory.

The women in boxy white hats, the sorcery powders and oils running in the drains, flung from the stalls by the indignant prophet stalking through, all sorcery gone underground into the earth, from which it will have to be refined yet again. Now I itched to read, as if I had only to blow the dust off the chiselled words. She came in her black suit, like a graphite star, the Mistress of the House of Books. I would have her in the organ loft while the sixteen-foot bourdon vibrated, in the space above the choir behind the false organ pipes where the natural wood boxes of deep notes were connected to their lung-machine like unvarnished coffins singing of the resurrection. The fish were rising to the rain. A woman singer was discussing their concert privately with the conductor, both unperturbed by the long stain of vaginal juice on the sheets in the unmade bed, from which they had just risen and which lay open like the book of the world. The thin answering rain like an echo rising from the flat rocks made of the drops shattered like fast-fruiting fountains.

The buttons like spiders spin the garment, and preside over it, hanging in their folds. They part the gossamer to allow the nourishing breast to protrude. There is the becoming part of feeding, and the dreaming part. Meals and conversation like dreams under a great vaulted roof, the nuptial mass where the young God consumes bread with his bride, and wine vivid as hymenal blood. The white bride throws off her white veil to feed, she is a young black virgin: ebony, ivory and musk.

The great Punch-and-Judy show of the thunderstorm with its arching rainbows created by lightningflash; knock Judy-cloud on the head and the tears fall. After, unclean waxy daylight of the town smelling of deodorants, the daylight wax before work, before the air runs shuddering in hot exhaust fumes. He rubs his penis with her blouse to start the day right, for she is away; the odour of warm silk and girls: thus she returns like a bee into the wax, nibbling it and erecting chambers of six sides in all the indifference.

I sent a perturbation out to him; he looked up, the natty clergyman. Smell of old people like bonfires in autumn, balsamic dry foliage. Your three daughters giving off smells of supple leather, chamois and horse-saddle, and living horse-skin, while Einstein stands on a bridge over the little river watching in the water reflections of curved space, and crowds pass by unnoticing.

The musicians all decently clad in Golly-cloth. A rotting figure in the cellos. An odour of hot silk from the shirt-fronts. In the churchyard, an awareness of all the dead holding their breath in expectation of the resurrection. The creepie-crawlies sidle off the bone and prepare to devise another figure elsewhere, of wings and sunshine, of eggs and insect dew. The quartet fiddling away at the poolside, and the pulse of the waves there rocks the water in its square basin, the motion left in it by one boy doing a bump-jump; and on that motion many swimmers rest and listen to the music on their backs, the heads cushioned on the water, the throats relaxed into the entire stretch of the body, everyone aligned with the pages of water so that they can enter them without a splash, the music suddenly shut off and replaced by the bass hum of the green pool as you swim downwards into its tune with your eyes open. Wetting the head changes the mood, the glittering divers emerge, hair spiky like a different forest of aerials on the roof, the mind changed as by wireless.

Under the black light, mother and daughter, in Poldark Mine, near Helston, the room lined with shelves full of the crystalline minerals bathed in ultra-violet, shining their unnamed colours, like solid fireworks slowly exploding, the mother and daughter, the faces black but the radiant white calcite of the teeth luminous as the million year lump of calcite aglow beside them, the light's tunes played on the rocks, the nails bright in the black hands like night reaching out of the bluely-luminous ocean-foaming sleeves.

This autumn I noticed the wasps eating a toad flattened by cars on the road, they were tearing away strips of leather. I noticed a dead mouse with its stringy fur and the wasps all over it like a magnificent yellow-black brocade, epaulettes, decorations, moving fruit. I saw them pinching crumbs out of a dog-turd, nipping up little blood-and-wood loaves off a butcher's gut-stained sawdusted floor. I was caught in our mother the rain, and still the wasps came weaving to taste and carry away lichen from the bark of the tree under which I sheltered. I thought they were a kind of electricity, attracted by charges. I wondered how they would bask in the presence of a whirling dynamo, painted in yellow and green. I thought they would mulct it of its grease, and touch down on the shining spinning shaft, electric wasp licking up the honey of machinery.

Spread out the lace to let the ghosts escape. I walk dripping; I was caught in our mother the rain; I shine with it. This wood is as full of ghosts as mother's lace. The trees make a great hand to touch the child. Look, there is a black rabbit under the hazel trees, it seems to beg. Walking with his aura alight and in touch with all he passed, it sent its colours back to him like feelings, his skin the radio. Cat and mouse sharing the same hole.

The Seven Stars of Ursa Major were the skulls of seven smiths who had been raised to the firmament, still tapping and twinkling with their hammers. A human can dance and sing until beauty is present, or pound iron. In the dark there is a resurrection of eyes. The loose clothes create electricity and phantasms. There is a doomsday wolf fettered by these smiths to the Polestar, they are in constant attendance on his chains.

Come, O Friend, let us welcome the Bride! We have given bread to the well and taken omens from footsteps. The king goes with lifted head to the Holy Lamp. O my beloved, how sweet it is to go down and bathe in the pool before your eyes, letting you see how my drenched linen dress marries the beauty of my body. Come, look at me.

The ship-shape burial mounds. Utensils that beckon to others and to the unnamed senses. I feel I have turned the earth itself from Falmouth to Exeter, the journey was so long in the rattling stage-coaches joined end to end. I pass the places where the water has devoured, and the places of I-Dea the inward Gs; there is secret teaching in the underwater palaces.

In Trinity College Chapel the organ vibrated like a river through the inner space pretending to be sound-love. It smelt of the organ, this chapel. I intuned through my nose to counter its influence. A harmonious factory a possibility? The factory the shattered man's organ. The factories that have been invented in the chapels! Like roaring love-waters in the ears. The earth shifting, the tiles crackling instantly with the music's patterns, they have to set clear tiles every year, as a bow on the edge of a plate of glass tuckers the lycopodium into standing waves. A factory of standing waves. The waves standing like great invisible personages each of which is a full choir. The armed rapport.

Armed rapport. Her shirt a bottle of vapours labelled with a yoni-triangle, which is also a linen bottle with a lip for pouring, a curcubite that charges its own scents with heartbeats, and puffs them out in soft panting. The high-style suit, the white blouse and the throat radiant with pearls, a sign of the presence of wedding fairies, the salient throat; gloves held like hypnotised doves to display the discreet nudity of hands; Rose Mary, Ros Marina, dew of the sea, which settles on all the turf as the pearls settle round her throat.

The Hallow E'en stakes. The middle-aged man who smelt the moon, its perfume as it rose and set, its altering odours as it waxes and wanes. It is the same religion when people claim they can feel the serpent's slow movements through their feet as they stand in the ancient shrines, where the dead Osiris is shown as the Still-Heart, a mummy, dead and yet alive.

Cat and mouse sharing the same hole. Dragons weary of battle. Phoenix playing in the cinnebar crevice. Donkeys in the Third Moon of Spring. A flight of seagulls playing among the waves, in the spray from the crests. A sparrow picking out grains of rice. The manner in which large stones sink when thrown into the sea. The manner in which a snake enters its hole when about to hibernate for the winter. The abyss sensing everything.

Great empty reverberating powerhouses disguised as college chapels. They shiver the bad man to bits, the good man to bits. The bits vainly try to rejoin calling it 'science'. He opened the door of room ten on staircase B and found a banqueting hall. Somebody was rehearsing his speech: many people naturally enjoy abstracts: suits and ties for example, or watching the quilt and cento of meadows from a plane. I listened on; his speech was like the weather, the electrical clouds altering my mind, sometimes opening it as in answer to prayer, sometimes closing it with bloody and balsamic images.

The Fool resurrected with a mysterious elixir: The Golden Frosty Drop. Eros is the serpent desire that flies through the air. The electrical clouds altering my mind, sometimes opening it as in answer to prayer, sometimes closing it, bloody and balsamic. The first mysterious act, as the blue darkens, as the mood darkens, like a tear-drop on a blue shirt; and with an alteration in the air, a condensing of the whole scene.

The pope made saints out of rich witches, but poor witches were burned. Convent witches were canonised also. Women ...in whose drowsy minds the devil hath got a fine seat. An old woman with feet like unto a wheel of fire. Scatter the ashes; if they stay all in one place she can rise again. The wheel-goddess of cyclic and deepening time, of the maelstrom, the dancer of the fairy wheel, she who turns the year, the Ferris Wheel, the Fairies' Wheel, the Celtic Star or Wheel of Arionrod, not the day of judgment but deepening judgment, not last judgment, not last illness but return to illness, return to health, not one person but thirteen, the outer coven reflecting the inner zodiac. A linen-goddess, a woman, a rider of the wheel, of pre-Christian fairy folk whose souls were involved in Karmic cycles depicted in the dances.

Slogans, jokes, drawings and tic-tac-toe crowd the walls of little white rooms with no furniture together with obscene poems and pithy aphorisms. But she had been out in the sunny air. Indoors as she spoke to me I smelt the fresh landscape from her lungs, as though they had become sunlit fields, the beautiful day had been photographed in its perfume in her lungs, and she now smelt of it, it spoke to me in the darkened bedroom, her thymos, her smell, her soul. And at other times she brings the starlit night into the early morning bedroom.

The lost work of an illusionist. Not lost. Passing. His gauzes and theatrical veils. Mists, milk of water flying through the grasses. The teats of the sky-cow. That aches the bones, that disciplines the thoughts. His treasure-chests suddenly opened on light, after ordeals, the young assistant lost in the cabinet, pierced with swords, no blood because he is missing, and then he leaps out of where he could not have been, studded with an arrangement of jewels, the Greek name for which is kosmos. His ordeals, the bullet caught in the teeth, the knives snatched out of the air, and returned, the trombone that echoes up to the clouds creating thunder. All turned to weather. His dress suit separates into cotton fibres, his flesh sublimes off the bones, the clouds of his flesh separate, and he comes through the mist as a spirit, as a spirit; spiritual transformations were the purpose of his pantomimes from the beginning.

In the afterlife a gardener goes on gardening, but he is not a gardener only, but a garden. The angel of all the roses brims over the garden wall. I heard the crunching of numberless feet along the radial paths. On the skyline he was nearly invisible in his blue clothes. And the drunken servant goes on descending, ascending the cellar steps sipping at the decanter, and the soul of the wine embraces him from the damp earth floors of the tuns. It is like the smell of a mother's early-morning arms. He sets the rose in motion; the other carries the warm red wine into the garden in a rose-stem glass and they both toast the angels. Their bodies give off a potion of scents like a herb-bed of flowers in a sudden shower of rain.

The ghost of a frock. The endless trains of the ghosts of toilet-paper. She uses her frock as toilet paper. A paper dress will do for a ghost. She grins, and I see the shit under and within. I see through her into the shit. Maggots prepare to gain wings and fly. When matters look this way there is no need to exclaim otherwise. These visions which are roused in the earth by the chafing of the sky. And the resurrections: the stones lie overturned as the forests do. The dead live in the trees until it is time to come forth. For every dead person there springs a tree. It is their home, an opulent one, a very opulent palace, this tree given by earth, air and rain. The green leaves cover the shit. A green papery dress. The forests seethe in their maggot.

Under the face of the Bat, life lived, the flittermouse whose face is a cross between a baby and a dog. Under the Bat, her shadow etched against the moon. The doctor sings the bat into his living-room, the singing doctor. Perfect love and perfect trust has grown between them. The bat exudes a little semen for the doctor's potions. The doctor takes the pulse of the bat before waving him farewell. The doctor is a cross between a man and a serpent, and his alliance with the delicate membraneous skinny creature is strong. He pours a glass of twelve hearth whisky for them both. Four fingers.

The higher the cloud the colder it is, and the louder the thunder, says the Smiling Host at his white portals; I have given you the attic. The walls were trembling, and as I entered, merely entered, the thunder gave a soft preliminary rumble outside in the broad windows where I saw the air-streams mixing lubriciously. It was not, as they used to say in my childhood, the clouds knocking together, not exactly that: it was the air-masses wrestling, whistling skin gliding over whistling skin, silk over silk, and silk over warm glass or over sulphur globes, as in the old electrical experiments, creating electricity and vast jumping sparks. This toil went on all over the world above our heads, and beneath our feet too, for the static charges of the earth moved under these influences in their rock reservoirs, as the sea under the wind. And we, the children? In my attic window, I was staring with wide eyes straight into the processes of the angels, and of the unconscious mind, the objective psyche, the turmoils and beauties of the spiritual world, the respiration of the Goddess.

After sex the woman goes about the house, singing. She sets the rose in motion. She sets the house in motion, she stands gliding, the rooms revolve around her, she is the centre. We do not go upstairs; the stairs travel downwards on command under our feet. The smell of a mother's early-morning arms. The perfumes of the bed transmitted about the house by the great gasps and billowings of the blankets in bedmaking. They practised yoga until beauty was present. We both occupied the form of a woman. Her body gave off a sudden potion of scents like a herb-garden in a sudden shower of rain. A woman like a magnetic wave, the crest of her hair. The invisible body which accompanied her. The pocket full of posies: the cave of underground flowers, the perfume of the earth, the underground fairyland. As it travels under our foundations reflecting the clouds above, our house is set in motion around the centre where I penetrate her nature; her body, the house-body filled with our ghost, set into perfumed resonance. The pyrosome of love-fire, wildfire.

The three grandmothers under the earth who cause floods. Doomsday by water. As she left us, the tension from the thundercloud grazing the land lessened. We lifted our glasses and took a drink. The two, man and woman, with their clothes slightly out of phase, a small gender-shift, and in the colour, heterodyning. She occupied the form of a woman, but she was the thunder, and she sets the cave of flowers in motion. A white cloud enters, like a marble reclining figure of the Bard, with his fringes of hair drifting about his ears, reclining on his elbow. A strange shining taste in the hall for three days after. The smell of mother's early-morning arms. The unsmiling animal at her heels. The kaolin tips like great land yachts. They practised yoga and coitus until beauty was present. A great cumulus system sailed in like kaolin yachting in the sky. A cloud like the Bard leaning on his ear, a reclining figure. The electricity ran down his legs like warm piss. As she decided to say goodbye, the tension from the cloud floating above like a slum tenement grew less. The inductance between us caught from the cloud and increased, but amplified the feeling of weather and wet ferns. The winds rushing into the low pressure zone, building electricity in magnificent columns. The trees could breathe, and formed their soaring temples on the foundation of their foliage. A priestess sacrificed perfume on every leaf.

As she left us, the tension from the thundercloud grazing the land lessened. We lifted our glasses and took a drink. The two, man and woman, with their clothes slightly out of phase, the two differing human shapes, heterodyning. The pocket full of posies, the cave of flowers, the underground fairyland, the shades within the soil moving with the clouds. The rose sets the thunder in motion. Earth and sky moving together, arms linked. The child within, the secret sharer, knows the clouds in its astrodrome, watches the dragonish shapes. She occupied the form of a woman. She was for that moment the thunder, behind the door with the skeleton door-knocker, the bones hold a sword in their left hand and wear a triangular skirt of silver. Her witch-name was Vesica. As I touch the fixed star of her clitoris, her body gives off a potion of scents like a herb-bed of flowers in a sudden shower of rain. A woman like a big magnetic wave. A standing wave which keeps its shape but exchanges its substance with its surroundings continually. A strange shining taste in the air. The scent of the stone pines, like the moon's grove of the zodiac which she passes through at night.

No body was found in the tomb; only the phantom or shade was found there. Allowing the spirit to escape so that it can balance the waters and nourish the fields. In one of the hells the shades are seen burning, but these were able to resist the fire, and it is consequently said 'The shades live; they have raised their powers' in the crucible of the house of flame. The solstice in December, Yule a mother of smells. The great theatres hidden in the moon and the clouds. The great schools of dancing. The midges show it, the spirits dance in everything as the great round shining arena passes overhead.

Neither needing nor casting a shadow. Her black hair spreading in the water like a huge flower. To go into control – meaning to go into spirit-control. The bucket of black tin-sand, the black gold of Cornwall. It shifted a spectrum of ruddy iron-ore across its black surface as he shook the bucket, a ghost of rust, a wine of the surface, a spectre of pocket-knives. Control. The winter winds low like cattle in the disused mines.

Their faces could be seen for ever in the markings on the panther, or all-beast. The faces of the slain host are seen in the markings on the moon. They raised their priestly power by burning witches. The great cloud of blood and cannon smoke, the thunder clouds over battlefields like armies marching away, the cannon-rumble of thunder. The battle now is always there. The cloud radioactive with a noise like typewriters. The thundercloud sealing Falmouth in behind its hills. The planetarium above, minor clouds float reduced in this vapour, the planets wheel in immense clouds over our heads. Were that leaden cloud to blow away you would see Saturn a few miles over our heads; in that sunset-vapour Mars; in that light rain Venus and in the feathers scudding in the rain-puddle, Mercury.

We go to bed in our outdoor clothes. So we can be shopping while we're sleeping. Or in our garden clothes. Then we can be growing and planting. In boiled shirt and puffed dress. Then we come dancing. In khaki gear so we can fight and make up after. In lamé underwear. To glitter like a pop group and dream like videos. In labyrinth checks, to wander among the horses, the dressage schools, the rousing bets. We do not sleep in top hats. Or in welders' masks. Though football vests help us score. And cricket shirts to play the game. We do not use medals which scratch the chest like nails. Or in our shrouds, though lace and tapes delay us. Above all we do not use pyjamas. Or retire to sleep in nightdresses. All the world should feel relaxed as bed. That is enlightenment. But not pyjamas, above all. Not pyjamas.

The company who make nylons, who clothe the legs of women in shiny electrical sheathing, who insulate the legs in plastic, they also with similar resources make atomic bombs. A noble earthquake, a noble earthquake! he cried as they detonated the nylon stockings; it awoke him in his Yosemite log cabin. He wished to study the daily aftershocks that grumbled through the sierras, so he placed a bucket of water on his table to observe the sloshing. The silk stockings kicked the world, the smoke went up like the earth drawing off a stocking and tossing it aside. The bucket sloshed to its dregs.

Equivalent times tend to be proportional to the fourth root of body mass, so that time goes 10 times as fast for a 30 gram mouse as for a 300 kilogram cow: lifespan, gestation period, protein turnover, breath duration, and pulse interval: the five vital airs. So the mouse fits as many breaths and heartbeats into its short life as the cow does into its long one. The broken water in the Roads that heralds the Vernal Equinox.

A magic Yule. The women and children are excited by their presents. Their pine tree working with their perfume. As Santa passes from person to person giving out presents he takes up a sniff of perfume from one, and then the next, it adds up in his lungs to a total Christmas. Each one like a little scented ornament hung on the one total spiritous household tree. Hung like glowing stars on the pine tree of my lungs. The Christmas tree the outer lungs. A good Xmas the right blending of smells: the father working so hard at the presents to get the right smell off his family; the mother blending in the kitchen her right smells so their juices rise; the parcels and presents, open them and you give off little squirts of envy-gas.

The women dressing like the weather and the seasons to bring the mind into accord with the climate, all the looms constructed in compliment to the weaver of the firmament. The planetarium of the skin, the stars rising across it and tracing their meridians. The slurry of mines, the shadow of landscapes. You look down the shaft of the ankh and see the great stone at the end, in the chamber beyond the cross-roads.

She had been out in the fresh air, hanging clothes on the line. When she came indoors, I smelt the fresh landscape as she exhaled it, the countryside streaming in her breath, through the parks of her lungs smelling of fields and fresh washing. The women dressing like the weather and the seasons to bring the mind in accord with the climate. Blue and white like summer skies; blowing skirts printed with all flowers in spring; fruits and rusts of autumn.

The five vital airs whisper and speak. Hell is other people. But, in Hell, you meet such interesting people. Yet, if you are interested in people, you are not in hell. G. Christ, plumber of the saturnine. His clothes are his attitude to work, the denim, the blue and white of the clouds. Like the clouds condensed; by his work he condenses the clouds into sweat, which stains the sky of his clothes darker, like a storm. Then he must strip them off, and bathe his skin luminous again. The other blows the great trump. He is the herald, dressed in the dragons of the family lands. The clouds rise over the estates in the form of coiling dragons. The herald blows his trump, and they descend returning as rain, and fertility. He is dressed in the sins which kept the land in equilibrium. The broken water in the Roads which heralds the vernal equinox. And the drinking: to swell oneself with drink, to become sensitive as a swollen balloon squeaking to a thumb, and a tightly blown rubber, to become, like the forests, moist, like the women premenstrual.

The sharp stimulus of frankincense, which is as if all the trees of paradise were burning. The fragrant portals of flame and smoke. The Ayr in God is a lovely pleasant still breath. Or voyce blowing. The Original of the Ayr (in which the Holy Ghost riseth up) is the exit going forth of the powers, or their moving. And the water in God is also of another kind: it is the source or fountain in the powers, and it is not of an elementary kind, as it is in this world. It is most like the sap or juice of an apple, but is very bright and lightsome, like heaven. It is like a flame, but cooling like water, and fragrant.

The bed scented the entire house. The name of Virgo as a constellation meant 'furrow'. Its star principal, Spica, was called in Babylon 'the corn-ear of the Goddess Shala.' Familiar mysticism, living by the field of wheat at Budock. That sea of wheat, the bands of shadows gliding across it from the road to the footpath. She walks it with her throat bare, familiar. A luminous vulva at the throat folded of cloth, pretending it is not that. Visible everywhere. The women maintain their power by emphasising such functions. The string of beads taps against the luminous collar, like a small overture of drums. The skin's speech rises from this flue in warm convection, filling rooms, or uncoiling down the path, mingling with the speech of the wheat. She smiles at me just as if everything were going on, which it is. This is why they talk over tea-tables, to mingle scents of tea, cream, jam, and people; this is why we must speak fair words in such places, they smell sweet. Do not look down your nose at such gatherings. The bed scented the entire house, like a den of winged lions. It has thereby a thousand doors through which the stars can shine. He devotes his hours to writing words of exactly that rhythm and accent that can evoke the blessed breeze from her body. Stars principal.